Making Room

MANDY MILLER

Contents

Dedication

To Jack – Thank you for being "my one" and helping me make room for all the fun, joy and love this life has to offer and reminding me to live life to the fullest, to cherish each and every moment, to take risks when needed, and to be myself while dreaming big all along the way.

Preface

I wanted to take this space to share a bit about how this novel was created and about how my process works. As I listened to a song by Ashley Cooke, as weird as it may sound, I could just feel a book take form inside of me. I came up with my characters and some things about them and then the title, Making Room, came to my mind. I am also an artist as well as a writer, so the term "making room" made me think of a studio. As I began thinking about the title and the story line, I began to think of the main character as going through major changes in her life. Not only would she make room in her life for the important things, but she would experience living her life out over the next year almost as a painted canvas being changed into a masterpiece in the studio of a great artist. I also began to gather songs that popped into my mind because of their titles or lyrics. I then made a playlist that steers the story that I listened to while I wrote. I added new songs as the process continued. I guess I use songs as a type of outline, and those songs are meant to enhance the story like a movie's soundtrack. I have included the playlist at the end of the book, as well as a QR code because I think listening to the playlist would enhance the reading experience if the playlist were referenced by the reader as the story unfolds. Thanks for taking the time to read one of my stories. Enjoy! May it be a blessing in some way!

Note to Readers

T o all my dear readers— If you are just so busy you don't feel like you can even take a deep breath, please know you have options. Make changes!

May you make room to have joy, to connect, to find peace, to wonder, and to ultimately enjoy life. You've got one, make it count!

Love, Mandy

Introduction

As Dolly Parton once said, "Don't get so busy making a living that you forget to make a life." Well, that is exactly what Kendall Fitzpatrick had done. It was New Year's Eve, and she found herself reflecting on the past year, as well as surveying her entire life. At just 28 years old, she owned a successful art gallery and her own home in the suburbs. But what else did she have? Sadly, not much. She lacked a significant other, hadn't spoken to her best friend in years, and had not seen nor spoken to her parents in two years. Being an only child, she didn't have sibling relationships to contend with, however she did have a cat named Fendy, but *she* didn't require much attention. Kendall had always been a proud introvert who loved life and cherished her alone time.

Kendall didn't mind going to work before sunrise, working late every night, eating canned soup or cereal for dinner, and spending most holidays alone with her cat. Kendall had previously had a rather serious boyfriend named Colin but hadn't had much time to spend with him.

Kendall loved using her colored pens and pencils and all kinds of stickers in her treasured Erin Condren planner to keep her full schedule organized as she stayed eternally busy with important meetings and calls and appointments. She thought *that* was what made life worth living. She was known for putting in the work, and as a result, she was successful in the eyes of the world. She had all the right connections and attended all the trendy events to help her gallery and thus her career be a success, but she was also always in constant motion like a hummingbird in search of flower nectar.

Kendall was a beautiful petite brunette known for her style, her elegance, and her knowledge of contemporary art. Her clients, customers and her artists trusted her completely. *Architectural Digest,* along with many other popular art publications, interviewed her often through the years because of her keen ability to collaborate with top designers to find just the right art pieces to hang in the homes of the rich and famous.

Kendall was the apple of her parents' eyes and their pride and joy; however, she hadn't spoken to them in years. She was their one and only, so this had caused pain and awkwardness. When Kendall left for college, her relationship with her parents was strong. What happened, you might ask? Well, Kendall's mom became very ill due to complications with diabetes, and it frightened Kendall so much that she pulled away out of fear of losing her mom for good. Kendall was so afraid of loss that she was even afraid to *fully* live her life. As a result, she poured herself into her career and only her career. She knew how to grind, and she did it with gusto. And that is what she had done after losing her last two living grandparents within the last year.

Kendall's ability to hyper focus on work, however, wasn't always a good thing. That focus and drive had come between her and her boyfriend of three years just before Christmas. Kendall thought Colin was going to propose as they dined before her annual gallery Christmas party. Instead of giving her an engagement ring in a tiny gift-wrapped box, he had placed a key in the special box he had presented to her. He returned her house key, rather than proposing. It turns out that he was smarter than she imagined. He was smart enough to know that things with her would never change. Her career meant everything to her. Colin could never compete, and he knew that. To say Kendall was devastated was an understatement. She spent much of the holidays in bed eating toast, buttered rice and bananas to survive. It was sad to think Kendall thought her relationship with Colin was strong enough for Colin to want to propose. She was not just devastated at the time, but she had been oblivious as to how her full schedule affected her relationships, all of them. She thought she was thriving, but truth be told, really, she was barely surviving. She was all alone, with nothing but a business to show for her striving and grinding.

During the holidays, Kendall had received a Christmas card from her childhood best friend, Cait, which made Kendall question her own life decisions and priorities. Cait was already married and had just given birth to her first child. And Kendall had been so busy that she hadn't spoken to her friend since the birth of the baby and certainly hadn't been to visit Cait and the baby yet, even though they all lived in the same town.

That is why on this celebratory night of December 31st, Kendall found herself a bit lonely and alone with her planner and her cat analyzing her life and making lists--lists, not of resolutions, but of things she wanted to change about her life.

CHAPTER ONE

December 31

T he first thing on her list was "get to know the neighbors." Kendall had lived in her ranch house in the suburbs for four years, but she did not know a single neighbor. She usually left for the gallery at dawn and returned after dark. She was single and younger, and they were not. That is what she told herself to make herself feel better. She had been sick at home once before when Madge McCoy, a neighbor from across the street, rang the doorbell. Kendall had chosen to stay in bed and ignore the doorbell that day. "Things always seemed easier that way, until *tonight*" she thought to herself.

Kendall turned on New Year's Rockin' Eve and poured herself a small glass of champagne, then she sat down to complete her list. Kendall spent a few minutes thinking before writing anything else down. She knew things in her life had room to get better. She knew she had room to love and to connect more. If things were going to change, she was going to have to make changes. She loved who she was, and she was proud of what she had been able to accomplish, but she didn't want to get any older without changing some things. Colin leaving her made her wake up. She just *had* to prove him wrong. She *could* change and value other things, besides work. She just knew she could.

Kendall wanted to reconnect with Cait and meet her new baby, Harper. She wanted to go to visit her parents in Arizona. She wanted to discover a new artist to represent at the gallery. She wanted to hire a personal assistant, so she could travel if she wanted or needed. She wanted to start cleaning her own house and to let her expensive housekeeper go. Kendall was hesitant to write it down, but she *also* wanted to meet a man, not a 28-year-old boy like Colin, but a man who would love her like her father loved her mother if that was possible. She wanted to believe that it was indeed possible.

As she finished writing down her last item, Ryan Seacrest started the countdown on television. Before she took her first sip of champagne at the stroke of midnight, she added one final item to her list— "I want to be with a special someone this time next year."

Kendall tore out her list from her notebook, folded it, and placed it into her planner. She took her last sip, put her flute in the sink, and turned off the living room lights. "Tomorrow is another day and another year. May it be a blessed new year!" Kendall said

The List   December 31st

1. Get to know the neighbors.

2. Reconnect with Cait and meet Harper.

3. Go visit Mom and Dad.

4. Discover a new emerging artist for the gallery.

5. Hire a personal assistant.

6. Let Hilda go, so I can clean my own house.

7. Meet a real man that loves me like my father loves my mother.

8. Spend New Year's Eve next year with a special someone.

CHAPTER TWO

January 1

I t was New Year's Day, so the gallery was closed, and Kendall was home. She chose to sleep in because she was up late the night before. Sleeping in was a luxury she did not allow herself to indulge in very often. She had recorded several of her favorite movies and her plan was to stay on the couch snuggled under a blanket watching movies for the entire afternoon. She noticed it was 9:30 on her clock as she rolled over. Sleeping in for her was until 10 o'clock or later depending on the day. She hoped to make up for lost sleep.

As she closed her eyes and covered her head with her comforter, she heard the doorbell ring and a separate knock at the door. She tried to ignore it by covering her ears and squinting her eyes shut, but then she remembered *the list*. She moaned and threw back the covers, grabbed her robe and stumbled to the door.

She stood on her tiptoes and peeked through the peep hole in the door and saw a petite, older woman, so she slowly opened the door.

"Happy New Year! Larry and I noticed your car in the carport, so I wanted to bring you some of my breakfast casserole, to wish you a Happy New Year, and to invite you to a little lunch get together we have organized if you will be around about noon. Larry will be in front of the television watching his football games, but I've invited a few of our neighbor ladies I do not think you have met before if you would like to join us. Oh, I'm Peg Lawson, by the way. Larry and I live on your right. We drive the cream Camry and we have a white cat named Lacey. You might have seen her roaming the neighborhood or sleeping on top of your car sometimes. We get your mail by mistake sometimes, but we just put it straight in your mailbox because we assume you are one busy lady, and we do not *ever* want to *bother* you."

At noon, Kendall rang Peg and Larry's doorbell. Peg answered and welcomed her in the door and introduced her to Larry during a commercial as he sat on the couch. "You are the first one here," said Peg. "This is our New Year's tradition each year. Come to the table, and I will show you the spread. I'm a good 'ole southern gal, so I just must have black-eyed peas, cornbread, coleslaw, and ham for good luck and prosperity and blessings. What did you bring?" Peg said looking at what Kendall was carrying.

Kendall said, "I brought my famous strawberry cake. I make it often, and it was the only dessert I happened to have all the ingredients for. I hope everyone will like it." She looked up as the doorbell rang again. Peg rushed to the door saying, "It's got to be more of the neighbor ladies. I cannot wait for you to meet them."

Peg opened the door and welcomed Madge McCoy, Tish Parker, and Lucille Leone. Peg said, "Lucille lives to your left, Madge lives across the street from you and Tish lives up the street just around the bend."

"Nice to meet you all and Happy New Year," said Kendall.

Peg whispered to Kendall that all three women were single and either widowed or divorced. Then Peg announced loudly as she pointed towards her guests, "These ladies are our neighbors, but they are also three of my dearest friends. We do this every year, and we have been through all the ups and downs of life by each other's sides. Our kids also grew up together. To say we've been in the neighborhood for a while is an understatement."

"I am so excited you all thought to include me this year. I've been needing to get to know my neighbors," said Kendall.

Lucille said, "Well, you will find out soon enough. Everyone calls me 'Mama.'"

Peg explained, "Lucille has never worked outside the home, so she used to be in charge of our carpools and after school snack time for our kids while we were all still at work."

Tish said, "While I was working at the pediatric clinic, Lucille kept things calm and respectable here on Hanover Lane."

Madge quietly spoke up saying, "Yea, Lucille has been there for all of us in one way or another. She's a life saver, and she's got the wisdom of a woman twice her age. Kendall, if you ever need any advice, Lucille's expertise covers all aspects of life. She's a wise old bird, I'd say."

Peg directed all four of them past Larry on the couch to the dining table. Larry raised his arm and said, "Hi all! Good to see you! Happy New Year!" All three ladies waved and smiled at Larry while Tish said, "To you too, Larry."

Madge, Lucille and Tish placed their serving dishes on the table. Lucille brought famous meatballs. Madge brought a relish tray, and Tish brought broccoli cheese soup and homemade bread. Tish knew it didn't go with the traditional fare, but it was a neighborhood favorite. "Tish is known for her bread baking," Madge said. "I like to visit her just to smell her kitchen. She's always got something in the oven."

Peg said, "Ladies, I have dozens of cookies to share from the neighborhood cookie swap just before Christmas. Kendall, between those and your cake, all the guests are sure to have plenty of sugar to start the new year off right."

During half-time, Larry and the ladies filled their plates and sat down to bless the new year and fill their bellies. Larry didn't mind his time with the ladies because, truth be told, he liked to get the scoop on neighborhood goings-on. Larry preferred "goings-on" to "gossip." It somehow made him feel better about his sharing of neighborhood news.

Larry turned to Kendall and asked, "So dear, what do you do?"

Kendall began to explain, "Well, I own a small art gallery in the city called Gallery 116. It is my pride and joy. I help new artists get started selling their work in the bigger art world. I help them market their work by helping them share their stories of why they paint, and I help connect them with clients and patrons. It has been time consuming work through the years, but it is far more rewarding than hard work. I believe great art enhances lives. I see that happen every day at the gallery. I've met some great folks in my line of work through the years, as well."

"Where did you study and what did you study to do such a thing?"

"I studied art history at Yale, and I just decided to go out on my own and open a gallery shortly after graduating. I learned how to do that on my own along the way."

"Wow, we must head into the city sometime to see it and all the artwork you have available," said Larry.

Tish asked, "What type of art do you sell the most of at your gallery?"

Kendall answered, "Mostly landscapes and florals, but I do have a large client base that prefers large abstracts. Designers love the abstracts for color in the spaces they are creating."

Lucille said, "I don't doubt that at all. My son has a beautiful place in the city with walls covered in modern pieces. Abstract art collecting is one of his hobbies. He's an architect and the abstracts complement his design style quite beautifully. He seems to prefer pieces with lots of orange in them. For some reason, he always has. I wonder if he has ever been to your gallery before. I will have to ask him."

"Oh Anthony, we all love him! What a good kid!" said Madge.

"I know you have been closed some during the holidays. When do *you*, I mean *the gallery*, when does the *gallery* open back up?" said Peg.

"The third," said Kendall. "That gives me tomorrow to accomplish a few to-do list items here at the house before the work year begins. Luckily, work usually doesn't get too crazy until the spring. It should be a quiet few months of work before the busy season begins."

Madge and Peg both started speaking at the same time as they often did and then Peg took over saying, "We have loved having you with us today. It is nice to have some youth around here. We hope you have a nice day off tomorrow. We kind of highjacked your free day today. Thank you for the yummy cake!"

Lucille added, "Please don't hesitate to come knock on my door when you are home. I'm alone. I'd love the company. I can always fix us a cup of tea. And I've always got some scones to enjoy, as well. Now, I mean it! Take me up on it sometime! I've got a nice porch with an empty chair, and I'd love to have you sit in it. Oh, and you can officially call me 'Mama'. We know each other now."

Kendall, Madge, Tish and Lucille stood up from the table and Kendall thanked them all again, gathered up her cake plate and serving knife to head next door to watch her recorded movies. She had loved the conversations and the company, but she knew Fendy would need to eat, and Fendy might just enjoy some company too.

Everyone walked to the door, hugged and waved goodbye to Tish, Madge and Lucille.

Peg placed a hand on Kendall's arm saying, "Kendall, I know you've already gathered your things, but before you put on your coat, we were both wondering if you might have a few minutes more to visit. We know we commandeered your day, and it is getting late, but we wanted to chat a bit more." That meant Peg and Larry had news and gossip they wanted to share with their new friend and neighbor.

"I was not able to fill you in on the background of the neighbors before you met them today since it was such short notice, and actually I didn't really know who was going to make it today anyway. Larry and I were chatting earlier in the kitchen, and we thought it would be good for you to know some more information about our dear neighbors. They are all such kind people with a few having interesting stories that we wanted to share with you."

"First off, I know you heard us talking about Harry Fitzsimmons today. He was married to his lovely wife Mildred until she died of a sudden heart attack several months back." Peg continued, "She was one of my favorite people and dearest friends. Her passing really did a number on all of us. It woke us all up to our age and how delicate life is and to the importance of valuing relationships. Harry is a retired Air Force general. You would never know it because he doesn't share much about that these days. Harry is a true gentleman in every sense of the word. He loves planes, fly fishing and playing Santa for the neighborhood Christmas parties. Cora, his daughter, grew up here with our kids and she was always such a bright girl. However, she went off to school at Stanford and got mixed up with the wrong crowd, ran off with a guy, and left her parents in the dust wondering where their treasured daughter ended up. Mildred was just sick about her sweet girl."

"Before Mildred passed, Harry hired a private investigator to find Cora to help Mildred, but once they found her, she did not want anything to do with them. It was and still is such a sad situation," said Larry.

"Harry is a great person. If you can go visit him sometime, I am sure you both would get a lot out of it. He is lonely, and he misses his wife and daughter. I am sure he would appreciate a visit from someone other than us. Larry and I are always dropping in on him. He was supposed to come today, but he cancelled at the last minute. I think he is still a bit apprehensive about attending social gatherings without Mildred. He said he would just prefer to stay in today, and I told him we would all miss him."

"You met Tish today. She is another lovely person. Tish came alone because she is divorced. As we told you, Tish is the baker in the neighborhood. She bakes because she's a bit lonely. She bakes in her free time, which is every night after work and all weekend long. She says baking is her therapy and keeps her from needing medication. As she said, she works at the pediatric clinic. She still works there even though her ex-husband is one of the doctors. Somehow, they are still able to be in the same room together. They divorced because they grew apart after their kids left home. Her ex is now dating one of the receptionists, so we will see how long Tish lasts at *that* clinic. Tish has saved a few children at the clinic before. Those are wild stories. She loves to share them, so ask her about them sometime. Tish has two sons and a daughter. They all live in California. They went there to school and stayed, especially after the divorce. Apparently, it is hard for them to come back and to have to visit their parents at two different houses."

"Madge, oh dear, Madge, she is a character. She was always somewhat odd, but after her husband died of early onset Alzheimer's, she took it very hard, and it changed her. She has her memory unlike her husband, but some parts of her left when he did. She can be a bit paranoid at times, however she loves to wash dishes and to mow and to work in the yard and to help others however she can. Her husband, Derbo, had a huge coin collection when he was alive and now, she is always worried about someone stealing it. We have suggested she get a safe deposit box or many, if that is what it takes, to keep the collection safe. Every time she leaves the house even to work in the yard, she takes the collection with her. She even wears her robe to work outside because it has large enough pockets for all the coins. Madge is certainly interesting, but Larry and I do care for her a lot. She is a precious lady. She has no one in her family close by. She and her husband had one daughter, but she is a missionary in Uganda and rarely, if ever, comes home to see her mother. Madge tells me she does receive emails from her every three months or so. That is tragic, if you ask me," said Peg.

"Now, we have come to Lucille, or 'Mama' as we like to call her. Lucille was the on-call mother/babysitter in the neighborhood whenever anyone needed one. Mama never worked outside the home, but she *could* be an award-winning chef with her own restaurant if she wanted. Through the years, she has perfected her cooking skills, and she loves to share food with those she loves. Cooking is her love language. She prefers her own cooking, especially her Italian cooking. She learned to cook first from her mother and then from Lorenzo's mother. She says her cooking 'heals anything that ails ya.'"

"Lucille was married to Anthony's father, Lorenzo, until he passed away from complications from an infection after a simple surgery on his shoulder. Lorenzo was a renowned neurologist. He studied at Johns Hopkins. He had his practice here in town until just before he died. Lucille and Lorenzo only had Anthony because they lost a little girl when she was born, and Lucille had multiple miscarriages through the years. They had wanted a large family, but once they realized *that* wasn't in the plans, they poured their love into Anthony. She and Lorenzo treasured Anthony, and Mama still does. Anthony was devastated after his father's death. He almost dropped out of school at that point, but Mama encouraged him to keep going. She is proud that he graduated and that he became a successful architect after struggling so much after his father's death."

"Anthony also had a very serious girlfriend who was killed in a car crash years ago, but after learning from the death of his father, he pushed through the sadness and grieved and came out stronger on the other side. He has turned out to be such a great guy. He is kind, smart, successful and loving. He was and always has been a favorite "son of the neighborhood". We all love Anthony. I cannot wait for you to meet him. He will make a great husband and father for someone one day, at least we think so."

By the time Peg ended her speeches on the stories and lives of some of the neighbors, it was nearly five o'clock. Kendall gathered up her things *again*, put on her coat, and quickly jogged through the chilly evening air to get home as soon as possible.

CHAPTER THREE

January 2

K endall let herself sleep in late another day. It was 10 o'clock by the time she "stumbled into the kitchen" for her morning "cup of ambition" (For those who don't remember, that is what Dolly sang about coffee in her song "9 to 5"). Kendall allowed herself to have just one cup each morning. That was usually enough caffeine to keep her on task, and it would be today as she accomplished a few more items on *the list*.

At 10:30, she got up from the breakfast table to grab her phone. First, Kendall called Hilda to let her know that her services would no longer be needed. Kendall kept a spotless house anyway. She did not need to pay someone weekly to come behind her to make her place even cleaner for as little time as she spent there.

Hilda was disappointed, but she completely understood. Kendall assured her that she would pass her name along to the neighbors. Kendall had heard at the New Year get together that Harold Fitzsimmons had recently lost his wife, so she would mention to him and to the other ladies to see if anyone might be interested in Hilda's help. It was the least Kendall could do after letting Hilda go.

Kendall had accomplished another item on her list, now onto another. She not only wanted to clean her house before heading back to work, but she wanted to completely clean out her guest bedroom. She had recently read that if someone wanted more connections and people in their life, they needed to make room. She realized on New Year's Eve, that there was no room in her life—no room in her closet, in her bedroom, in her calendar, in her guest bedroom for anyone to visit, and ultimately in her life for anyone else at all. And she wanted to change that so desperately that her heart hurt.

So, she headed to her guest room with plastic totes and trash bags. It was time to get rid of old prom dresses, pageant dresses, cheerleader uniforms, sorority formal gowns, high school trophies and books she read once and would never read again.

She tidied up the desk area by making tax folders and throwing away old unnecessary receipts. She found a box of art supplies, opened them and arranged them neatly on the desk for when creativity might strike. Kendall was making room and setting up a "making room" just for herself. The gallery was for her artists, not for any of her art or anything *she* made. Kendall did need a space to create, however, because she was known to create when she felt inspired to do so.

She found old photos and a box of picture frames. She took a few minutes to put together some photos in frames to display around her home of personally meaningful memories—of her parents and her dear friend, Cait; of Fendy as a kitty the day she brought her home; and the framed Christmas card of Cait's family, including Harper.

Next, she headed to her own closet, clearing out old clothes she hadn't worn in years. She grabbed another standard pillow and pillowcase from her linen closet and added it to her bed. She also grabbed a small table next to an extra chair in her living room and placed it next to her bed, adding a lamp and an extra alarm clock, as well.

After grabbing some turkey salad with cranberries on Tish's shared bread, Kendall started some chicken tortilla soup for dinner, grabbed her cleaning supplies, and retrieved her vacuum from the closet and started cleaning her own house. She felt mature and satisfied as she finished up the cleaning. At five o'clock on the dot, the house was decluttered and sparkling and smelling like lavender, lemons and peppermint.

She returned to the kitchen and ladled up some soup and poured it into an extra-large Mason jar to take over to Mr. Fitzsimmon's house next door to Madge. She threw on her jacket, grabbed a few pieces of Tish's bread to wrap in foil and headed out into the dark wintry evening to meet another neighbor.

The ladies of the neighborhood had shared with Kendall that Harry was a bit slower getting to the door these days, so she waited as they suggested. When Harry answered the door after a few minutes, Kendall introduced herself, "Hi, I'm Kendall Fitzpatrick, one of your neighbors. I am so sorry for your recent loss, and I am also sorry and embarrassed that we have not met until now. I live next to Peg and Larry. I've been home all day, so I made you some soup. I attached a little tag to the lid with the recipe and the ingredients if you are allergic to anything," Kendall said handing Harry the soup-filled jar.

"Oh honey, I ain't like the kids these days--allergic to everything. I'm tough as nails. I could drink from the gutters and eat from the sidewalk and be all good. I'll only eat the soup if you stay and join me. I've been lonely lately. Television can offer only so much company."

Kendall agreed and spent the rest of the evening eating soup with Harry and chatting by his warm fire with a bit of gin and whiskey.

"What a gentle and kind man! And what a blessed and meaningful three days I had without ever even watching those recorded movies," Kendall thought as she crawled into bed that night.

CHAPTER FOUR

January 3

Kendall woke up thinking about what Harry had said about his only daughter, Cora. He said she hadn't been back to see her parents in six years. She had gotten involved with a boy in college who did not see eye to eye with her parents. She had chosen to move in with the boy and to carry on with him, never speaking to her parents again. Cora had not even known about her mother's death. Harry had no way of contacting her. She could tell by the look on his face and the tone in his voice that he was devastated by it all. The worst part was that he had no way of making any of it better. He was now living with the effects of his only daughter's choices, and it broke his heart, and it had *literally* broken his wife's heart.

The next morning Kendall drove to the gallery with a heavy heart, not being able to get Harry, his daughter and his wife out of her mind. Kendall could not wait to get to work because as tough as life was on the human heart at times, she knew art could always help troubled hearts heal.

As soon as she unlocked the gallery, however, she started singing the song, "Back to Life" by Soul II Soul and her mind started racing with all of the things she needed to accomplish on her first day back to work after the holidays. She thought, "I sure wish I had an assistant that I could spout off my lists to. I feel like having someone else at the gallery might help me feel less stressed and overwhelmed." Then, she remembered another thing on *the list*. Kendall ran to her office computer and immediately typed a job description on a popular new employment website. She hoped that she just might have a new helper by the end of the week if she were lucky. She felt like the new year might be the perfect time for someone to be looking for a new job. She was hoping for a kind office assistant with just a little knowledge about the art world or at least sales, in general.

Next, Kendall got out her artist files and her yearly art show file. She had some serious planning to do. She would start her day establishing the show date and then begin contacting all of her gallery artists. She would also need to design invitations and to let all the local publications know that she had an opening for a new artist, since Judy had decided to hang up her brush for now.

Kendall got out her planner and looked over her desk calendar. She usually had the show in April because that gave her artists three months after Christmas to create a new series or a selection of paintings, which was plenty of time for *her* artists. She decided on April the 16th to give the artists maximum time, and it would give her plenty of time to notify and invite all her clients and customers and new contacts. Also, her designers loved an April show because it gave them new pieces for their summer projects after buying their winter art and other supplies at market in January. She appreciated her designers. They kept her up to date on all the latest trends and styles in the design world, which changes more than those in the art world.

At noon, just before heading out to grab a salad and a smoothie for lunch, she received her first application from a recent college graduate in town. There was hope she would get a good response from her open-position listing. As she locked the door and flipped the closed sign, she smiled to herself and began singing "Changes" by David Bowie.

When she got back from lunch, she began contacting her artists. It was the first year she wouldn't be contacting Judy, and she was sad, but she knew Judy was enjoying her retirement with lots of travel.

The first person she contacted was Branton Fletcher. She had not talked with him during the holidays because she knew he had been traveling considerably. She had tried dating Branton once, before she made her rule of never dating her artists. He was a great person, a great artist and friend, but not dating material for her. He loved the transient, do not settle anywhere for too long, lifestyle. He had that kind of a vibe, and he was proud of it. His work was always beautiful, however. He painted mainly detailed landscapes of mountains and the streams that run through them.

His work was not local, although his studio was. He painted what he encountered traveling the world, and Kendall loved every piece he painted.

Kendall was contacting him first because he showed his work at other galleries. She didn't receive all his work. She knew she had competition, and she did not want to miss out by not letting him know when she needed pieces and for what dates and events.

As he answered the phone he said, "Hey, Doll, what's going on? I've missed you. How were your holidays? Mine were swamped with travel. I spent Christmas with my sister in Colorado. You wouldn't believe all I have planned to paint."

Kendall said, "That is why I'm calling. I assumed you might have some fun things planned that my clients will be thrilled with. I'm just letting you know that the spring art show will be on April 16th. I have space to hang anything you've got for me before then too."

"I'll drop off a few small studies I did of the Rockies. Also, I have a beautiful one of a couple fly fishing in one of the streams I happened upon on one of my hikes. It's pretty good. I'll probably recreate it on a larger scale."

Kendall said, "Please drop it by and paint a bigger one; I have just the person in mind for the smaller one. I will just buy it outright and give it as a gift. It will be perfect. Just call before you drop by to confirm that the gallery will be open. I let the weather make the hours sometimes this time of year."

"Will do, Deary. I'll chat with you soon." Branton said as he hung up.

Before her next call, Kendall checked her computer. She had two more applicants from two men in the area, but with no experience. Because their wording seemed fishy and questionable, Kendall thought that their emails might just be a scam.

The next call Kendall made was to Leslie Cantrell. Her call immediately went to voicemail, but Kendall was not surprised, so she left a voicemail with all the pertinent information. Leslie was a truly skilled abstract artist with a huge fan base with five kids. When her kids attend school, she paints and never answers her phone. Therefore, Kendall was accustomed to catching up with Leslie in the gallery on her delivery days.

Inglewood Fleming answered her call on the first ring. Inglewood was so thankful to have Kendall represent him, that he treated her like a boss and a princess. He respected Kendall for all her success, even if she was fifteen years younger than him.

"Good to hear from you, Madam. How are you? What can I do for you today?" he said.

"I'm just calling to give you the dates of this year's show and to see what you have on your plate this year," she said.

"Well, I'm thinking about concentrating on portraiture this year. I can do commissions if you like, as well. As far as pieces for the show, I recently decided to paint the faces I came across while living in India after college working for the Peace Corps. I have beautiful photographs, and I've already got some stellar paintings that I've painted from those photographs. Everyone seems to be brought to tears when they see them, if that tells you anything. I have some very detailed still-life pieces I have been working on too that could be of interest to some clients."

Kendall expressed how excited she was about his pieces and assured him she would drop by his studio to see them on Monday.

The last artist Kendall needed to reach out to was Susie Eubanks. Susie was her go-to floral artist. She could paint the most beautiful and unique floral pieces that Kendall's collectors and designers just flipped over. Her collectors love the colors she uses in her pieces, both soft and relaxing and intense and vibrant. Kendall's customers purchase Susie's paintings for gifts and as investments intended to be passed down from generation to generation. Susie has an eye for framing her work, as well, which adds to the beauty of each creation.

Susie was excited to hear this year's show dates. She painted most of the year with Kendall's show in mind. Susie was always painting if she wasn't back in Alabama visiting family. She told Kendall that she already completed ten pieces designated for the show and that she was almost finished with the two commissioned pieces for Kendall's customers. Kendall was also checking on those commissions.

"I will be finished with the second commission by the end of the week, then give me a week to let it dry and to get it framed. I can deliver it by the first part of February, if that works."

Kendall said, "Sure! That is perfect! My customer is giving his commissioned piece to his wife for Valentine's Day, and the other one is a piece my client commissioned as a birthday gift to herself. Your pieces are so meaningful and lovely. Everyone wants them for themselves. Because of that, I never get to keep them hanging for long when I do get some in for the gallery. I'm going to need to commission one specifically for myself and the gallery just to be able to keep one of your pieces permanently."

"Well, I already have some ready for the show and plenty for the gallery now. I was painting instead of baking this past holiday season. I'm ahead of myself and my yearly plans," said Susie. "I'll drop them by when Joe gets our Tahoe out of the shop."

"Thank you so much for painting so much for me, Susie. I cannot tell you how thankful I am. I cannot wait to let your collectors know that we have new pieces on the way. I know they will be thrilled."

Kendall hung up with Susie, stood up and headed to the office kitchenette to fix a cup of hot tea to help with her afternoon drowsiness. All her sleeping in during the holidays didn't help much on this "get back to work" day.

It was already 4:30, but she did not close the gallery until six, even in the winter. She sat down with her hot tea and opened the app to create the gallery show invitation. It would take time to get them in and to get them all mailed out, so she wanted to at least get the designing part completed before the end of the day. As she began the invitation her computer beeped with an email notification.

It was an email from an applicant, a Reign Gardener. She had not gone through the website channels, so she must have looked up the gallery and the owner and confidently contacted Kendall directly. Kendall found that initiative extremely impressive.

Kendall could not wait to email Reign back. She sounded like an interesting possibility, but Kendall decided to wait until the next morning to contact her. She spent the drive home thinking about Reign's mentioned experience and the questions she would likely ask her.

Reign's email included her attached resume. On her resume she listed a degree in interior design and her work experience at an on-campus art gallery. Her duties there included assisting with acquiring acquisitions, helping with show installations, and with planning special gallery events. She also mentioned in the email that her mom is a personal organizer and that she has her mom's genes for giftedness with all types of organization, which Kendall thought might help her out quite a bit. Since leaving the gallery at her college, Reign had been working for her father's law firm as an executive assistant and front desk attendant. She mentioned that she was looking to put some space between her career and her father. Kendall would be sure to ask her about all of that tomorrow when she planned to call her for the first time to possibly set up an in-person interview.

CHAPTER FIVE

January 4

K endall was up early and in the gallery by seven. She decided to make her call to Reign at eight, so she had an hour to proofread the invitation from the day before and to get it ordered.

Kendall dialed the number at 8:01. Reign answered the phone shocked and a bit sleepy sounding, "Hello, this is Reign. May I ask who is calling?"

"This is Kendall Fitzpatrick from Gallery 116," said Kendall. "I am sorry to call so early, but I got your email, and I was so excited to have a chat. I couldn't wait any later."

"Oh, I'm sorry I sound a bit sleepy. I am normally at work by 7:30, but my father's office does not open back up until January the 9th, so I'm not working this week. I just got out of bed. I am, however, so excited you are calling. I am really interested in the position you have open. I think I am highly qualified."

Kendall asked, "Why are you looking to move jobs? I saw that you are working for your father presently."

Reign explained, "I love my father and I have enjoyed working at his office, but my passion is not law. I'm interested in design and art and organizing, a bit more like my mother. My skill set is more along those lines. I figure my father can easily find a very qualified replacement for my position at the firm. An opportunity to work at a gallery like yours does not come around that often, for sure, especially in the city."

Kendall then began asking a few questions of Reign, "Do you live in the city or in the suburbs? About how long would it take you to get to the gallery in the mornings and home in the evenings? Are you looking for a full-time position?"

"Yes, I would like a full-time job. I want to be able to support myself completely. I am 28 years old, so it is time I stopped leaning on my dear old dad, even though I have been helpful to him and to his partners, and he has been kind enough to give me a job. I live a few blocks from the gallery, within walking distance for sure," said Reign.

Kendall asked if Reign had any time to meet at the local sandwich shop during lunch for a quick in-person interview. She promised to walk her back to the gallery for an official tour afterwards even though Reign had said she was familiar with the gallery.

Kendall arrived at The Bakery Bun a few minutes early and then Reign arrived right on time just minutes later. Kendall recognized her the minute she walked in the door. Reign was dressed in a classy black jumpsuit with her long blonde hair pulled up in a ponytail with sunglasses on her head, heels as tall and skinny as toothpicks and carrying a black and gold Hermès bag. She was a beautiful girl and Kendall knew she was a girl no one could forget. She certainly hadn't forgotten her once she saw her again, and she said so as soon as Reign walked up to the table.

"I have seen you in the gallery before. I could never forget a face like yours. If I remember correctly, you bought one of Susie's paintings for your mom a while back. You must have paid in cash because your name did not ring any bells when you emailed."

"I did. My dad sent me to the gallery with business cash. It was a partner gift to my mom for all of the party organizing she has handled for Gardener, Franks, and Halston. My mom is one special lady, and she loves Susie's work, so it was the perfect gift."

Kendall and Reign continued their interview over a lunch of winter squash soup in warm bread bowls topped with warm toasted pepitas and lemon ginger iced tea to drink. They chatted about the position requirements and the duties that it would entail. They talked about Reign's ability to arrive early to open the gallery each day and for days with iffy weather since Kendall had such a long drive in every day. They talked about the gallery, their lives, their cats, and their lack of romance and love. At the end of their time together at the restaurant, it was evident that they had truly hit it off. They had things in common, and they were already on track to become fast friends. The only thing they didn't discuss was their love for fashion. Kendall could tell Reign must be obsessed with fashion because of the way she was dressed.

Before leaving the restaurant, Kendall walked back up to the counter to order them each a warm chocolate chip cookie and hot tea for the walk back to the gallery.

Kendall opened the door and turned over the open sign as she said, "Welcome to the gallery, my home away from home, my little baby." Kendall showed her around pointing out the work of all of her main artists. Kendall explained that all the empty wall space was from Christmas sales. She assured her that she would either be picking up new work or that the artists would be delivering plenty of pieces to cover the empty spaces within the next several weeks or sooner. Kendall showed her the back office with plenty of room to add another desk if Reign decided to take the position. She took her to see the office kitchenette, and then she showed Reign the art show invitation and both of her sacred calendars/planners.

Reign assured Kendall that she would have no trouble opening the gallery, helping her hang artwork, and keeping her life and gallery in order and running smoothly. Reign was very confident about her own skills and her ability to do just what Kendall wanted and needed. Kendall talked over salary numbers and offered Reign the job. They discussed Reign starting as early as Friday. Kendall was ecstatic about what this arrangement was going to do for her, for them *both* really. Reign seemed to be excited about starting a real career out from under her father's wings. Reign had also mentioned looking forward to spending every day with Kendall, someone she could see as her future boss and eventually a best friend.

Kendall walked Reign to the door, shook her hand, and then gave her a big hug. "See you Friday, Reign, at 8 a.m. I'm excited and looking forward to working with you," Kendall said closing the door. She had a few more chores to do before heading home for the evening. Since Reign would be working at the gallery from now on, Kendall knew she was going to be able to take some days off to visit Cait across town to meet Baby Harper and to travel to Arizona to finally visit her parents after several years.

Kendall walked back to the office, sat down at her desk, and stared at her desk calendar for a few moments. She had set the dates for the gallery show, hired an assistant, fired her housekeeper, met some neighbors, and now it was time to contact her parents and to let them know that she was finally available to visit them in Arizona. It was going to be an awkward call because it had been so many years since she had even spoken to them. She was always too busy with the gallery as sole owner to ever get away, and she let that excuse keep her from calling. Kendall was ashamed and embarrassed, but the call had to be made. She had to do it, so she picked up the phone and began to dial their number.

Kendall's dad answered the phone as Kendall said, "Hey Dad, it is Kendall! I know it has been forever since I picked up the phone to call, and I'm sorry. I am calling now not just to say, hello, but to tell you I'm planning to fly out to see you and Mom in May just after my big gallery show if that works for you guys."

"Well, I'll be Kendall, I can't believe it. You know your momma is going to be thrilled. Let me get her. She's gonna want to hear your voice, and she's gonna love hearing your news. She sure misses you, Dear." Kendall could hear her father yell for her mother, Joan, to come to the phone.

"What is it, Honey? Why are you yelling my name, Arthur?" Joan said.

Arthur replied with excitement, "Come answer the phone someone special is on the line, and the person wants to tell you something!"

"Hello?" asked Joan cautiously.

"It's me, Momma, Kendall!" she said.

"Well, gracious me, Kendall. I haven't heard your voice in years. How are you? How is the gallery? Are you healthy? Are you busy? Boy, your dad and I sure do miss you and your smile. We miss hearing how things are going. Are you still dating Colin? Or is there someone else special in your life? How is Fendy?" Kendall's mom said inquisitively.

"No, Momma, I'm not dating Colin anymore or anyone else. I've been too busy to pour into relationships lately, but Fendy is still alive and thriving I'm proud to say," Kendall said.

Her mom quietly added, "I sure hope you can make room for a few relationships. My relationship with your father and my relationships with my friends get me through both the trials and the joys of life. I sure want you to experience those kinds of blessings, not to mention kids one day. I know you do not like me bringing these things up, but a mom can dream, can't she? Kendall, I want you to know that you are in my prayers every night whether we talk much or not. You will always be my precious little girl, grown or not."

Kendall added, "Thank you, Mom. I am calling to let you and Dad know that I am making plans to visit you both there in May just after my spring gallery show."

"Oh darling, that is the best news I've heard in years. We cannot wait. I'm going to start planning our menus tonight. I want to take you to the cutest boutique while you are here. I know you will love it. I will let you talk back with Dad. Give him the exact dates, so he can put them in our calendar on his phone. Thanks, Baby Girl. I love you so." Joan said as she handed the phone back to Arthur.

After a few more minutes of chatting with her dad, Kendall hung up with tears in her eyes because she finally had a first week of May trip to Arizona planned and also highlighted in her planner.

She had one more call to make before calling it a day. It had been a very busy, yet truly successful day. She dialed Cait's number by heart. Cait was married, but she and her husband were still living at Cait's parents' house. She had been dialing that number most of her life, although not so much lately. Cait's mom answered and quickly handed the phone over to a shocked Cait. Kendall could hear Harper crying in the background.

"Hey, Cait, it is me, Ken, how are you?" Kendall said.

"My stars, Kendall, I cannot believe it is you. I have been trying to reach you for a while now. I left a few messages for you at the gallery. I was hoping you would get them there."

Kendall explained, "I did get them. I have been meaning to call you for months and then the holidays happened, but that is another story. Your baby! I cannot believe you had a baby! She is beautiful! I loved the picture on your Christmas card!"

Cait said, "Well, I called a few times because I've been wanting you to meet Harper, and I wanted to be able to see you before we move."

"MOVE?" Kendall shouted into the phone. "You aren't really moving, are you? You can't. It won't be the same without you here. Why are you moving anyway?"

Cait said with a giggle, "Come on Kendall! Why would it matter if I moved? We never talk anymore. You are way too busy for me. I had a baby months ago, and I never heard from you. Cait could be heard sniffing in the phone. Kendall knew she was crying. Cait was being honest, and it hurt Kendall's heart.

"Oh, Cait! I am so sorry. I have been a terrible friend. Do you have time to see me at all before you move?" Kendall asked.

"Yes, I do. We are not moving until after St. Patrick's Day," said Cait. "We are moving then because Toby works for Comcast, and he is moving to their headquarters in Philadelphia, and they don't need him there until the end of March. We have already found a house, our first house, that we will move into about a week after we get to Philly. That will give us a few weeks to get settled before he reports to his new job. We would love for you to come over sometime to meet Harper. I know my parents would love to see you too. You were always their favorite out of all of my childhood buddies."

Kendall and Cait set a time for Kendall to visit the next week. Kendall closed her planner after crossing two more tasks off *the list*. Kendall enjoyed chatting with her parents and Cait. She was thankful that they had made it on her list and that she had made it a priority to follow through. She was excited to head home for dinner and bed. She knew she was going to sleep well because she hired Reign and she was starting soon, and she had finally reached out to her parents and Cait and those three things had been on her mind and on her invisible to-do list for a while.

Kendall's heart was happy and blessed and she couldn't wait to tell Fendy all about why she was so happy when she saw her at home. She closed and locked the gallery in the freezing cold night air, walked to her car, scraped the car's windshield, then opened the door and slid into the driver's seat while turning on her favorite podcast for the forty-minute drive home. She was thankful that she had her kitty and some leftover chicken tortilla soup and strawberry cake waiting for her when she got home because it had been a long day, and she was looking forward to a little comfort.

CHAPTER SIX

February 12

J anuary ended up being a typical January at the gallery, however Reign had started working there and that had changed
everything for Kendall. February came in with a bang, however.
The weather had been rather dreadful, even for winter. February
the 11th was their fifth big snowfall of the year. The gallery was
only opening on time on the 12th, thanks to Reign. She had
great snow boots and a super warm coat, and she was making the
four-block walk into the gallery. She had been opening for Kendall
most of February after Kendall had given Reign her own key at the
end of January. Reign had proven dependable and trustworthy.

Kendall had woken up extra early that morning with a call from Jean Bingging. She was one of the owners of Poodely Poodely, a pet salon and spa next door to the gallery. In previous years, Kendall had been available to open the spa for her on bad weather days. Since Reign was opening for Kendall due to snow covered roads, Kendall had to tell Jean that she would not be in the city early enough to help her out. Jean was very disappointed because her clients started dropping off their dogs at 7 a.m. Jean explained that her other partners, Patricia Pollygum, and Hazel Higgenbotham were unable to get out of their driveways, so they too were unable to help. Jean ended up deciding to call her clients to cancel instead of opening when she could get there. She thanked Kendall anyway and got off the phone to start making her client calls. Kendall felt guilty, but she hated to add "opening Poodely Poodely" to Reign's early morning gallery duties that morning in particular because their day was already scheduled to be a busy one.

Susie Eubanks was the first person to show up to the gallery that morning after Reign opened. Reign was ecstatic to meet Susie in person because she had heard all about her from Kendall, and she was certainly familiar with her work.

Susie's husband, Joe, drove the Tahoe right up in front of the front door to make it easier to walk her pieces into the gallery. Reign made sure to put salt on the sidewalk out front as soon as she had unlocked the door that morning, so their artists and customers would have a safe pathway to the door across the sidewalk.

"Hello, Reign, I am Susie Eubanks. I am so happy to meet you. Kendall has told me all about you and how much you have helped her already in just a few short weeks. I know she must really appreciate you on days like today. I talked to her before coming in. She thought she would not make it until closer to eleven, and I do not believe she is in, is she?"

Reign confirmed to Susie that Kendall had not made it in yet and said, "She told me on the phone this morning that because the roads in the suburbs were so much worse than those in the city she would be in late again today. I'm sure Kendall will be sad she missed seeing you. However, I am so happy to get to meet you. My father's company purchased one of your pieces for my mom. She is a huge fan of your work. What have you brought for the gallery today?"

"Well, I have the one commissioned piece purchased by your client for his wife right here," Susie said handing over a framed 9x12 piece wrapped in brown craft paper. "I have the other commissioned piece in the car and four others for the gallery that Joe will help me bring in after I let him know to start hauling them in here. I sure do like painting, but this part is not my favorite, especially on a day like today," Susie said putting her gloves back on and squeezing her shoulders together pretending to freeze.

Joe and Susie began bringing in the pieces. Reign kept the other commissioned piece wrapped up until Kendall could check it out, but as they brought in the gallery pieces, Reign unwrapped them and leaned them against the wall where Susie's other work was hanging and where there were open spaces with room for hanging. Reign and Kendall were going to have lots of pieces to hang by the end of the day if all the pickups and deliveries took place as scheduled.

About 9:30, Leslie Cantrell pulled her family van right in front of the door, blocking the sidewalk completely. Reign had not met her, but Kendall had told Reign to expect her sometime that morning after dropping her kids off at school after a one-hour weather delay. Leslie ran into the gallery with workout clothes on splattered in every color of paint imaginable announcing her name and why she was there. She dropped off two very impressive geometric abstracts in green, coral, navy and tan. Reign thought the pieces were spectacular and she knew enough about her work to know that her pieces would not last long once she and Kendall hung them on the wall. She had seen the wait list for her larger pieces. It was over two pages long. Reign did not know yet how Kendall decided who got the first call to see Leslie's work.

Leslie quickly dropped off the pieces, leaned them against the front wall and yelled as she exited the door, "Thanks Reign! Nice to meet you! Have a good day! Tell Kendall hello and that we can catch up when I drop off the other big piece that I am almost finished with. Got to get home to paint! School is in session!"

Reign went back to her new desk in the back office to do some research on up-and-coming artists for Kendall, while she ate her morning yogurt parfait with homemade granola and fresh blueberries. She was deep in her research when she heard the front door chime signaling that someone had entered the gallery. Reign rolled back her chair and stood up just as a beautiful tall, dark and handsome man poked his head into the office door. Reign jumped back completely startled because she had never had a customer come all the way to the back office to search for her or for Kendall. Most customers just waited patiently out front.

"I am so sorry that I startled you. I am looking for Kendall. Is she here today? I made sure to call yesterday to make sure the gallery would be open, and she assured me she would be here. I am Branton by the way, Branton Fletcher, the artist."

"Ohhhh," said Reign. She did tell me you were dropping things off today, but she did not know what time. The gallery has been slow this morning except for artists dropping off work, so I thought I could sneak in some computer work waiting on Kendall to get in. I am sorry I was not out front and all the way back in the office when you arrived. I am Reign, Reign Gardener. Nice to meet you, Branton. Reign could hardly make eye contact with him because of his blue eyes and his astonishingly good looks. Reign swallowed hard and eked out another question. "What have you brought us today?"

Branton said, "Why don't you walk with me out front, and I will show you? I brought in one piece already, but I need to go out to my truck to get the others. That is unless you need to keep working."

Reign immediately followed him out to the front of the gallery. He had already placed the small framed 8x10 of the couple fly fishing on the front counter. The minute Reign saw the piece it took her breath away. The trees and stream were so realistic and majestic. It was captivating. It was like the couple in the scene had a special story to tell.

"Wow, what a piece!" said Reign. "It draws me in."

"Thanks! I painted it after returning from Colorado after Christmas. I happened upon that scene. It moved *me* then. I'm glad *you* like it. I think Kendall will too. I think she has it already in mind for someone. I'm thinking of doing a larger version if Kendall or my other gallery owners think they can sell a larger one.

I have two other pieces from my recent travels that I brought for the gallery too. I will run out now and get them."

Reign leaned against the counter and sighed and then spun around to release a bit of tension. She was mesmerized by Branton's presence. This type of thing just didn't happen to her. Most men typically frustrated her. She usually found them immature and arrogant, and they tended to act awkward in her presence, at least the ones that were attracted to her and vice versa. Branton was the opposite. He was confident and kind and seemed very respectful. She could not wait for Kendall to arrive, so she could get all the scoop on him, and she couldn't wait for him to walk back in the door, so she could get another glimpse of him. She was both shocked and surprised by her reaction.

The other two pieces he brought in were just as captivating, but for different reasons. Reign knew Kendall was going to be so excited that he was sharing these pieces with them and not with his other gallery back in Colorado. Branton left just after he brought in his pieces. He said to have Kendall call him on his cell when she got in. He left, thanking Reign for having the gallery open and for allowing him to interrupt her research.

"Thanks again! I hope to run into you here again sometime! I'm sure Kendall is excited to have you join her! I know I am." Branton mumbled the last part as he yanked open the stuck door making it chime again as he left. Reign realized she was never going to hear that bell the same way ever again. She knew she would spend the rest of the day picturing *that* face appear in the office doorway. Reign could not wait for Kendall to get to the gallery.

Reign called to get an update and an ETA from Kendall.

"This is Kendall. Can I help you?"

Reign said, "Hey it is me. Everything is great here. All of our expected deliveries arrived. I cannot wait for you to see what we received. When are you coming in?"

"I should be there within the hour. I was planning to stop by Inglewood's studio on the way in. He prefers me to pick out the pieces that I want, rather than having him drop off pieces he chooses. That arrangement seems to work for us. Will you be alright if I run and do that on the way?"

"Of course! I'm good here. I just have lots of questions I need to ask you."

"Go ahead! I'm just driving."

"Oh no I won't bother you now. They can wait until you get here." Reign did not want to upset Kendall while she was driving by asking personal questions.

Kendall walked through the front door exactly one hour later carrying two very special paintings—one was of the most angelic little boy on the streets of Kolkata and the other was a portrait of a mom and her baby on a bench in what looked like some type of park-like setting. Reign was so excited to start hanging all their new pieces that she got out the ladder and started doing just that five minutes after Kendall arrived for the day.

"How was Inglewood?" Reign asked climbing the ladder. She had met him before at his studio when Kendall took her along for one of her visits. She liked him and how appreciative he was of Kendall. "I love the new paintings you picked up from him today. I think he is on to something with those pieces. They show compassion like I have not noticed in his other paintings that I have seen."

"Yea, I think so too. I'm really proud of what he has been doing lately. How were Susie and Joe, and Branton and Leslie?"

"Well, none of them stayed long at all. They just dropped in and dropped off. And o.k., why did you not tell me about Branton before? I mean. What is he even?"

"What do you mean?" Kendall asked, staring at Reign looking across the gallery. "Reign? Reign? What do you mean? I told you *all* about Branton."

"Nope! Nope you didn't—not *all* about him! You never mentioned his looks, ever. How could you not? That is the *first* thing I would mention about him. He poked his head into the office while I was back there, and I about passed out. I was on my way to see who came in the door and the next thing I knew he was staring at me as he stood in the office doorway. *That* beautiful man was looking at *me*. I was so startled I could hardly speak. He thought I was scared, but I've never seen a more beautiful human in my life. And he was nice and kind. He wants you to call him by the way," Reign said a little frazzled and out of breath.

"Oh, I bet he does! Did you ever eventually calm down around him? Does he now think I have hired a lunatic? Tell me exactly what went down, so I'm prepared if he asks me questions. Did he drop off pieces or just stop by?"

"Oh, he dropped off pieces. They are amazing, and I told him so. I tried to be as calm and put together as I could be. I didn't want to embarrass you or the gallery. I know he shows at other galleries."

"Well, good!" said Kendall. "Where is the piece with the couple in it? I cannot wait to see that one."

"He put it on the front counter, and I left it there. He told me you wanted that piece for a gift." Reign announced as she hung one of Susie's pieces on the wall.

"I do!" said Kendall. I have a very precious neighbor that I met during the holidays that is from Colorado. I think it just might mean the world to him, so I'm going to drop it off to him after work.

After Kendall and Reign finished hanging all the new pieces on the gallery walls, they headed back to the back office. Reign wanted to get back to searching for new artists, and Kendall had to call Branton.

"Hey, Branton, this is Kendall. How are you? Thanks so much for the pieces. They are lovely. I'm giving the fly fishing one as a gift *tonight*. I will let you know Harry's reaction. I just know he's going to love it."

"Kendall, you know you are always welcome. Now, I do have beef with you though." Kendall's stomach turned. She was worried about losing Branton as an artist.

"Why in the world have I not met Reign before today? She is a true stunner. I think I scared her silly today though. Please apologize for me. I know we have a bit of history and I know Reign is your assistant, but may I please have your permission to get to know her better?"

"Of course! Just because we did not work out does not mean that I do not think you are a fabulous human, artist and friend. Reign is a great girl! I wish you lots of luck!"

"You may see me around there more than you like now, Kendall. I hope you can stand it," he said laughing as he hung up the phone.

As soon as Kendall hung up the phone with Branton, she yelled for Reign to come back into the office. She knew they didn't have a customer. Reign had just left the office to give her privacy for her call.

"Yes, Kendall, I am here. What can I help you with?"

"Reign, I'm not sure if you are ready for this or not, but I believe Branton was as taken by you as you were by him. He asked me for permission to get to know you. That might seem weird, but we are very dear friends, and he respects our working partnership immensely. I also must tell you that we did try dating back in the day, but we are better off as friends. Please feel free to date him if he asks you out. You are not going to hurt my feelings, and it should not have any negative effects on our relationship or my relationship with Branton. I want you both to find great people. He just might be who you have been looking for. It is the *love* month, you know?" Kendall giggled and stood up to stretch her legs and head to the kitchen for some tea.

Just as Kendall left the office, a call came into the gallery. Reign answered. It was Branton. He hadn't wasted any time. He called the gallery to get Reign's cell number and to ask her to dinner.

Branton said on the call, "It may seem too early to celebrate yet, but would you have dinner with me not tonight or tomorrow night, but the next night which happens to be Valentine's Day? I know it might seem like an odd night for a first date, but from what I experienced when I saw you in the gallery today, I think it *just might* be the perfect night for *our* first date." Reign agreed to the date, hung up and squealed like a girl who believes in love at first sight.

Kendall went running into the office to see what had happened. She was afraid Reign had encountered a mouse or worse.

"What in the world, Reign? I thought you were dying in here."

"Nope, I'm all good. I just answered the gallery phone and Branton asked me out. That is all."

"Well, I'd say that's a big deal. You're excited I assume. I hope so! Now, sit down here next to me we have got to accomplish more today than hanging paintings and handling phone calls. I need your opinion on a few things for the show."

After working in the office for a few more hours, Kendall packed up her bag, grabbed Branton's painting she was giving to Harry, told Reign she was leaving for the day, and headed out. She assumed that it might take her a while to drive back to the neighborhood on roads that were beginning to get slick again as the temperature began to drop. The change in weather was sure to add to her drivetime, and she was trying hard to get to Harry's by 7.

Harry answered his door at 7:10. Kendall wasn't that much later than she told him she would be. She was hoping to stop by her house first to feed the cat, but she knew what time Harry went to bed and opted to stop by his house first.

"Well, Howdy, sweet girl! It is great to see your face! How was work?" Harry asked as he opened the door.

"It was great! I don't feel like I was there that long today. I didn't start the day until much later because of the snow. I now have an assistant that opens for me when I cannot get in early enough. She has been amazing, and she has been exactly who I needed to hire to help me keep the gallery running smoothly."

"I know you told me you were going to come see me, but what brings you here?"

"Well, I have a little present for you that I thought you just might like. The minute I heard Branton was painting it I thought of you. It is my special gift to you," Kendall said as she unwrapped the painting and handed it to Harry.

The minute he saw it tears filled his eyes and ran down his cheeks. He could not speak for a good five minutes. He just sat in his chair admiring the painting.

Kendall finally said, "I know you and your wife used to live in Colorado, and one of my artists just got back from there and painted this piece upon returning."

"How did you know? How could you know that Mildred and I loved to fly fish? We also had a little stream on our property. This looks just like us in that stream. Oh, Kendall, this is a treasure! I am so thankful you thought of me and that you took the time to stop by! I know you know I don't have many people left in my life that would do this for me. You have blessed me more than you know tonight, last time you stopped by and every time I see you or hear your voice. Thank you so much, My Dear! Now, you have had a busy day. You need to get home to feed your cat, and I need to get to bed. Mornin' comes early when you are my age, you know?" Harry walked Kendall to the door, gave her a big hug and a kiss on the cheek, and waved goodnight to her as she quickly jumped back into her car to head home just across the street.

CHAPTER SEVEN

March 15

M arch arrived with much wanted milder temperatures. The gallery had been hopping with customers, and the girls were busy with planning and with interviews relating to the upcoming art show. Since Reign's Valentine date with Branton, Reign and Branton had been inseparable. This really surprised them all. Branton indeed was around the gallery more than ever before and seemed to put his world travels on hold for the time being.

Kendall enjoyed seeing her friend often, and she was so excited to see Reign so happy. Kendall *wasn't* in love, but she enjoyed seeing love blossom before her eyes.

"Kendall," said Reign as she walked into the office, "I was wondering if you would like to go to dinner with me and my father at his club, Pine Valley, tomorrow night. My mom is out of town with some of her girlfriends, so it will be just my dad with us. He has been wanting to meet you. It will be a pre-St. Patrick's Day special menu which my father thought you might like, being a Fitzpatrick and all."

"Sure! That would be wonderful! I am finally heading to visit my friend, Cait, tonight. And the day after tomorrow we are still on for drinks at Mulligan's, correct?"

"Yes, we are! Branton will join us that night if that is o.k." Reign said.

Kendall said, "Sure! I wanted to see if you would be all right if I leave around one today. We do not have much on the schedule. I want to spend as much time today as I can with Cait and the baby. Before I leave today, I would like to make our plane tickets to New York. The sooner we get to see Trixie and her studio the better."

Reign had discovered a new artist with all her research and with Branton's connections too. Her name is Trixie Dixon, and she lives in Brooklyn Heights, New York. Kendall had contacted her and obtained images of all of her latest work. The plan was for Reign and Kendall to close the gallery for one day only. They were making the trip to see her studio and work, in person. Trixie is a young artist, but she is one of the leading artists in the return of figurative art. Apparently, artworks with strong references to the real world are making a big comeback, and Kendall wanted to include some examples at the gallery for her clients, especially her designers.

Kendall left just before one o'clock to head across town to see Cait and Toby and Harper and of course, Cait's parents too. She was looking forward to it, but she was a bit nervous because she had not seen them all in so long. Kendall listened to the "Footloose" soundtrack on the way because it always reminded her of Cait and their many good times.

As she pulled up in front of 607 East Magnolia, tears appeared in her eyes. Kendall didn't know how many other times she would visit there again, but she remembered how many times she had walked in that front door to pick Cait up or to stay the night for a sleepover.

Cait's mom, Gloria, answered the door and gave Cait the biggest hug. Cait's father, Frank, said as he walked to the door, "Well, Kendall, you pushed it to the last minute, didn't you? They are moving the day after tomorrow."

Kendall shyly admitted, "I know, sir. I have been very busy at the gallery."

"We know you have, Doll. We know what great friends you and Cait used to be, and we know if you had had any extra time, you would have made your way over here before now."

Kendall's heart sank. She had been busy, but she knew she had not been *that* busy. She certainly could have *made* time just as she had today.

Cait came running into the kitchen carrying the baby followed by Toby. "Oh Ken, I have missed you so. Please let me introduce you to Harper. She is the best baby!"

"I would not expect anything else. She is absolutely beautiful! May I hold her?" Kendall said holding out both arms. Harper leaned over toward Kendall as if she knew she was her mom's best friend and someone who could be trusted. Kendall and Cait talked about old memories and Toby and Cait's plans for Philadelphia while Toby and Cait's parents set the table and finished preparing the feast for dinner. Harper seemed delighted to be in Kendall's arms, and Kendall loved every minute. She could not believe she had waited so long to reconnect with Cait and to finally meet Harper. Motherhood looked good on Cait. Toby seemed happy too and confident the move was for the best. Cait's parents agreed. They were going to miss them, but they knew it would be good for all three of them to get out on their own in a totally new town.

Kendall apologized for not being there during and after Harper's birth. They cried together, and Cait told Kendall how sad she was that they were just now getting together.

Kendall said, "You know, I was thinking, Cait. You can make new friends every day, but you sure can't make old friends," because Kendall loved Dolly and Kenny's song about the same thing. "We are old friends and again I am so sorry. I truly cherish you and I have not shown it. I know you will meet new friends, but I will always be here for you."

"Oh Kendall, you have always been my best friend, and you always will be! I know you are just now meeting Harper, but would you consider being her godmother? She has your middle name as her middle name. She is Harper Ruth after you. We wanted to tell you in person that is why you are just now hearing this. Toby and I both agree that there is no other woman in both of our lives better for the job. We might not see each other all of the time, but we will be back often to visit you and my parents. We will make sure that you are always a part of her life. That is if you agree, of course."

"Oh Cait, I am so honored and of course I will agree to be Harper Ruth's godmother," Kendall said smiling and crying happy tears.

After a feast with a table full of comfort foods like mashed potatoes and macaroni and cheese and corn casserole and pinto beans and a roast and homemade rolls, Kendall thanked Cait's family, for a lovely evening, gave them all hugs, and kissed the baby on the head.

Kendall said, "I still have the same number. Call me anytime to tell me about the move and to let me know how you are settling in. Safe travels! Thanks again for everything and especially for welcoming me back into your life, Cait, my dear friend! Again, call me anytime, if you need anything at all! Love you so!"

Kendall waved as she pulled out of their driveway and drove back to the gallery. It was already closed and a bit late, but she wasn't too far away and had a few things to do that couldn't wait until morning. Since she never got around to booking their flights earlier, she logged in quickly and booked the flights for the next week. The sooner they signed Trixie, the better. She left a note on Reign's computer letting her know the booked flight information and then headed home to Fendy. That night had been a late night, but the next two nights were sure to be even later, so she was heading straight to bed to get her beauty sleep.

CHAPTER EIGHT

March 16

K endall woke early as usual, but it wasn't her alarm that woke her, but the beeping of the trash truck backing down the street after gathering the neighborhood garbage. After getting all dressed for the day and packing an extra outfit for dinner with Reign and her father, Kendall was ready to head into work. As she stepped out into the carport, she could see Mama Leone in her robe awkwardly trying to roll her garbage can back up the driveway. Kendall felt sorry for her. It was cold out, and Mama had on a robe and house slippers.

Kendall yelled across the yard saying, "Mama, I can get that for you! Leave it right there! I'm on my way!" Kendall made her way across the soggy, wet grass in her heels to drag in the can for Mama. Mama was embarrassed to be seen in her robe struggling with something so silly.

"Darling, I've got this! I do it every week. I'm just sorry you caught me. I can usually get the can in before anyone sees me, or at least I think I've been able to do that. No one has mentioned it if they have seen me. You did not have to come over. You look so fancy dressed in work clothes for the gallery. You shouldn't have. However, since you are here, want to come in for a cup of coffee or that tea I promised you? I've got both, and a scone too. I've even got a travel cup that you can take with you if you are in a rush."

"I think I've got a few minutes to chat. Just let me make a call to my assistant and let her know where I am and when to expect me. I couldn't ask for a better way to spend my morning."

Kendall removed her heels and followed Mama into her house. Her house smelled like peach cobbler and toasted almonds. It was neat and tidy and cozy with the television on one of the cooking channels. Mama was a sucker for a good recipe, so she watched hours every day taking notes along the way. She had a red spiral notebook and her favorite pen by her chair to prove it. Everywhere Kendall looked there were framed photos of a very handsome man. Kendall did not think the photos were of Mama's late husband because most were recent photos or so they appeared to be.

Kendall had to ask who the man was after staring at his pictures while Mama fixed their coffee and scones. Mama brought in Kendall's coffee and a plate of scones saying, "I know it is weird. I'm Italian, but I just love my scones. It is o.k. to borrow pastries from another culture, right? I mean it is bread, and I love me some bread!" Mama said sitting down on the couch next to Kendall.

As Mama sat down, Kendall blurted out and pointed her finger around the room, "Who is the gentleman in all of these photos?"

"Oh, that is Anthony, my son! I think Madge mentioned him the first day we met."

"Oh, yes, your son, the architect, who lives in the city! I remember!" Kendall said blushing and thinking about how attractive he was in every single photo. "Something did look a bit familiar about him. Maybe he had been in the gallery before," she thought to herself.

Mama said, "Yea he is the one who loves abstract art. I never asked if he had been to your gallery before. I've got to do that! Anthony is my best boy, my only boy, my only child. I do love him so! He loves the city, but I tell him all the time that it just isn't the place to raise a family, not that he even has a girlfriend. I mean he has *had* several girlfriends, but no one Mama approved of, if you know what I mean. He is 30 and happy with his life, or so he says he is. You kids these days do not think much about marriage. I, on the other hand, value marriage and see its purpose in making a life beautiful. I do not know what kind of life I would have had without my marriage to Anthony's father. We loved each other so much and we had a great time every day of our marriage, and I am not kidding you. Every day was truly magical. It gave my life meaning and joy and I miss him every single day, especially on trash day," Mama said laughing out loud and cracking herself up. "You are a busy girl; don't you wish for a serious someone to come home to at night? Is your cat enough? Is your career enough? Are you lonely or happy and content?"

Well, a few months ago I might have answered your questions differently. A lot has happened since New Year's Eve. I began analyzing my life and asking myself those questions. I now have an assistant that has become a great friend, and she has recently fallen in love, rather quickly I might add. However, she is so happy, and I have realized after watching it happen firsthand that I am a tad bit jealous of what she has found. I just saw my childhood best friend yesterday, and she is married and already has a child. It kind of made me question my choices and decisions that I had been so confident in and proud of for so long.

"Well, that is actually a really great thing to do. Take stock in things. I just do not want you kids to miss out on anything trying to pave new paths and leaving tradition in the dust. There are so many blessings with marriage. I don't believe it is an archaic outdated idea. But that is just Mama's opinion."

They had been talking for two hours when Kendall finally glanced at her phone. "My assistant is going to wonder if I'm ever going to make it in today. I have loved every minute of our chat, but I must get going. Please let me help you get your can out and in every week. It will be my pleasure. I'm so glad I could help you this morning and that you invited me in. It has set me up for a great day. I can tell." Mama sent her off with a travel cup full of coffee and a scone to share with Reign. Mama was a delight, and Kendall was quickly learning about the joy and the value of neighborhood relationships.

Mama hugged Kendall as she left and said, "Come back anytime! You know I'll be here watching my shows and taking notes. Drop in! Next time, stay awhile longer! I'll be waiting!"

Kendall moseyed into the gallery at 10:30 with coffee in her right hand, a scone for Reign in her coat pocket, and her change of clothes on hangers in her left hand. The dinner was supposed to be a rather fancy affair, so Kendall brought a black cocktail dress and a light jacket. She planned to wear the same heels she wore traipsing through the yard to help Mama, so those heels just might need a little cleaning before dinner.

Reign greeted Kendall and asked where she had spent her morning. She explained who Mama was, where she lived, and she just might have mentioned her son's pictures too. Reign could tell by her description that Kendall was quite impressed by his looks, since she did not really know much else about Anthony, yet.

The day flew by. They had been swamped with customers looking for special pieces and late in the afternoon, Kendall had a quick phone interview from a local publication writing an article on the town's art scene and especially the upcoming show. There was buzz about the show, and she and Reign were quite excited about what it might mean for the gallery.

Six o'clock came soon it seemed. They closed the gallery and quickly changed clothes. They were meeting Reign's father at the club at 6:30 and according to Reign, her father was certain to be early and sitting at the bar visiting with his cronies when they arrived.

And that is exactly where they found him at 6:25 when they arrived. Their table wasn't ready, so they joined her father in the bar. He introduced himself to Kendall, "Hello, Kendall, I am Dean Gardener, Reign's dad but you knew that. It is so great to have you both join me tonight. My friends are going to see me with you two beauties and wonder what I'm doing." He then asked if the ladies wanted a cocktail before they were seated at their table. "I know you are Irish, Kendall. This is an early celebration night for you. Chris, our club mixologist, has designed some festive cocktails for tonight designed to go well with the dinner specials. If you are interested, go up and ask him about them."

Kendall headed up to the bar, chatted with Chris, ordered an "Irish Maid" and as she was waiting, Kendall glanced to her right and saw Colin, of all people, sitting at the bar with a girl. Her stomach dropped just as Chris handed her the drink. Then, Kendall's heart pounded, and her hands started shaking as she walked back to their table trying to carry her specialty cocktail. Colin had not spotted her, but Kendall wondered how she was supposed to act unbothered once she was back at the table. She could not let Reign and her father know what had happened, so she smiled, sat down, and acted like she had not just seen the ghost of a boyfriend past.

For dinner, Kendall chose corned beef and cabbage, not necessarily a sophisticated choice, but definitely one of Kendall's favorites. She was thrilled with her selection, and she was so thankful Reign and her father had invited her.

Dean expressed during dinner how thankful he was to Kendall for hiring Reign and for giving her a chance. Kendall assured him that she had given Reign more than a chance because Reign was worth *more* than a chance. She said Reign is essential and a rock star and that her talent and her skills are of immense value each and every day at the gallery.

Kendall enjoyed her night. She could tell that Reign had a great relationship with her father and that he had certainly passed down his style and elegance. Kendall was impressed by his gentle and distinguished demeanor. Just as the dinner conversation was winding down and just as they were about to get up out of their seats, Colin passed by the table and quickly locked eyes with Kendall.

Colin paused, then bent down to hug Kendall saying, "Kendall, it is so good to see you! What brings *you* here tonight? I have never seen you here before. Let me introduce you to Cornelia, my girlfriend," Colin said turning toward the redhead at his side while turning beet red himself. "Her father is a member here, so we join him here at least once a week."

"Nice to see you too, Colin, and it is nice to meet you, Cornelia! This is my personal assistant, Reign, and her father, Mr. Dean Gardener. It is my first time joining them here. Mr. Gardener and I had not met before tonight, but he thought the Irish fare would be something I just might enjoy."

Colin heard what Kendall said about Reign and he was very shocked that she would hire someone. In fact, he said out loud, "Really??? You hired someone to help you? I can't believe it, but I am happy for you! How is that working out?"

Kendall pointed to her dinner guests and said, "Doesn't it look like it is going well? Reign has been a life saver! I've changed a lot of things this year, or at least I'm working on it. I even contacted my parents and visited my old friend, Cait."

Colin knew what a huge deal all the things she shared were. He was beginning to think maybe he had been wrong about her. Maybe she did have what it takes to change.

Kendall could not stop staring at Cornelia trying to see if she could tell if they were serious or if they looked happier than she and Colin used to look together. It hurt her to see Colin with someone else, but it was good for her. He had moved on. She knew when she saw him that the feelings for him were gone, and that it was time for her to move on as well.

Colin gave her another hug and told Kendall to say hello to Fendy, and then he and Cornelia walked on to be seated at their table which was finally ready.

As they left the table, Reign looked at Kendall and said, "Oh my stars, Kendall. Was that *The* Colin? "I am so sorry you had to run into him here tonight." Reign's dad agreed. He could tell who Colin must have been, and he knew Cornelia and that she had a new boyfriend named Colin. "And, not to change the subject, but is Fendy *the* cat you always talk about going home to? Is it named after Fendi the designer fashion brand?"

"Oh no! I named her F-E-N-D-**Y**, like she "fends" for herself because I got her when I had no time and no business caring for anything else in my life. I think Colin mentioning Fendy was a bit of a jab because he always made me feel guilty for getting her in the first place. He felt I was being irresponsible."

Reign explained to her father, "Dad, Kendall has made some big changes in her life since the beginning of the year. We haven't known each other that long, but I am super proud of her! From what Kendall has told me, Colin leaving her was what kick-started the change."

"That's right!" Kendall said as all three of them stood up to leave. "Thank you so much, Mr. Gardener, for a wonderful evening! I am sorry for that little interruption at the end of the meal. Please forgive us for that. And thank you again for letting me steal your assistant. Reign is a true gem, and I can now call her one of my best friends. You raised one heck of a daughter!"

CHAPTER NINE

March 17–18

K endall woke up early, excited and ready to start the day. Last night had been fun, but today was a new day, a holiday. Kendall already had her outfit laid out. St. Patrick's Day had always been a big day in her family growing up, and she had always celebrated in her own way when she was out on her own. She had chosen an emerald, green turtleneck sweater, black straight-leg pants, and black booties for her day at the gallery. She had chosen green undergarments and socks too. She wasn't about to get pinched. On the way to work, she stopped at The Bakery Bun for fresh hot coffee and their specialty green frosted donuts to share with Reign and their customers. Reign had not been happy with all the goodies Kendall had been sharing lately, but it was a holiday and a green one at that. Kendall's favorite color was green, so green donuts were a holiday must-have.

Another day of work sped by. Reign had placed two orders for commissioned pieces, and they met with the caterer for the show. They also had a salesman drop by trying to promote a picture light with new technology. Kendall was not interested, so they quickly sent him away. For most of the afternoon, they watched the clock. Kendall and Reign agreed that closing time was not coming soon enough. They had plans to go out, and Branton was planning to meet them after work at Mulligan's Irish Pub for dinner. Kendall had a tradition of going there every year, and this year she asked Reign and Branton to join her. She wanted to keep the tradition, but she wasn't interested in going alone. They were scheduled to meet Branton at Mulligan's at 6:20. They were planning to have dinner before all the locals arrived for the official St. Patrick's Day Party later in the evening.

The girls arrived earlier, so they were seated and waiting at their table when Branton came in a few minutes late explaining the mess he had in his studio after receiving a damaged package containing newly ordered oil paints. He said he received the package at five and had to clean it all up and shower again after cleaning the mess. Somehow his apartment was *covered* in paint from one silly package incident. He was frustrated, but after seeing Reign's face, his attitude changed. He was smitten, and he couldn't hide it. The girls both ordered shepherd's pie and Branton ordered fish and chips. And, of course, they each ordered *just one* green beer to join in the festivities because they all had work the next day. They had just finished their meal after all their catching up when many of the locals started showing up yelling, high fiving, and chest bumping. It seemed a bit early for that behavior, but the crowd was obviously ready to celebrate. Branton and Reign and Kendall decided to stay seated for a bit. Their server assured them that they were fine to do so. Usually most of the crowd congregated around the bar anyway. They enjoyed where they were because they each loved to people watch. And a night for celebration like tonight was the perfect time to do so. The front door kept swinging open and letting in the chilly night air. On about the fifteenth time the door opened Kendall recognized a man's face walk through the door and immediately raised her voice and said whacking Reign on the arm, "No way! No way! It can't be! You have got to be kidding me!"

Reign freaked out and said, "What??? Not Colin, AGAIN!

"Oh no! It isn't Colin tonight. It is waaayyy weirder than that would be." Kendall took a deep breath in and let it out slowly trying to calm herself down saying, "That is *Anthony*—the guy in the white shirt over there to the left of the door. Mama Lucille Leone's son in the flesh, not in a picture frame. I am just floored! What even? Why? Why here? Why now? Should I go up and introduce myself? Would that be crazy? Will he think I'm crazy? He does not even know me. I know it is him, though. I would not forget that face and that body and Mama did mention that he lived in the city. What are the odds?"

Branton and Reign both agreed that she should at least walk past him somehow, sometime that night. They were not letting her off the hook. Reign agreed he was too good looking to not at least try something. They could both tell that Kendall was interested even though she did not really know him at all.

Kendall decided just to be brave. Anthony was Mama's only son. She had to talk to him for *Mama's* sake or at least that is what she was telling herself. Kendall stood up and walked toward Anthony with a smile on her face. Just as she was about to stop and say something, she smelled his cologne and Anthony caught her eye. Kendall got shy, put her head down and made a quick veer to the right to head to the bathroom instead. Back at the table Reign and Branton were cheering her on until her final move, and then they were crushed. But, then for some reason they noticed Anthony following Kendall to the back of the pub.

"What now, Branton? Should I go after her? Do you think she missed her chance? Why do you think he followed her?" Reign asked concerned as she strained to see through the growing crowd.

Branton said, "She's a big girl! I'm sure she will be fine. Just wait until she returns!"

A few minutes later, Kendall did return to the table a bit flushed, however.

Reign asked anxiously, "Did you talk to him?"

"I did," said Kendall. "He was so kind. He followed me to the hall outside the restrooms. He said he recognized me from the gallery. Anthony has apparently been to one of our shows. *He* recognized *me*. I told him that his mother lived next door to me and that she and I had become friends. He was completely shocked by that and by the fact that I had been inside his childhood home. He was very nice. Maybe you can meet him if he comes to the show in a few weeks. I did let him know that it was coming up, that we recently got in a lot of new artwork, and that hopefully we would be adding a new contemporary artist to the show and to the gallery. He seemed interested and excited to see some of our new work. We will see."

Well, I'd say that sounds promising on all fronts," said Branton. "You ladies have a busy day tomorrow. Are we ready to head out? All three of them stood up after paying the bill and made their way through the rambunctious crowd outside into the blistery night air. They hugged on the sidewalk just before Branton and Reign jumped into their Uber. Kendall then made her way to her car in a lot across the street. It had been a fun night, but she and Reign had an early morning flight to catch.

Morning did come early, but Kendall bounced out of bed. She and Reign were going to be gone for only one night, but she still had a bag to pack and a few things to do around the house before she began getting herself ready. Her shuttle to the airport was picking her up at six. She was planning on meeting Reign at their gate.

Kendall felt at peace when she finally saw Reign walking down the long line of chairs toward her at Gate C16 carrying two cups of coffee. Reign was a true assistant in every sense of the word, even on travel days. Kendall could finally relax as Reign arrived at their gate, so she took her paper coffee cup from Reign's hand and cautiously sipped it with a smile on her face and thankfulness in her heart.

They were expected to meet Trixie at her apartment, which was also her studio, before noon. They planned to visit, to get a tour around her studio, to choose a few of her pieces for the gallery if they were impressed by her work, to go out to dinner, and then to spend one night at the hotel. It was a quick trip in with an early flight back out the next day, so they would only have to close the gallery for the first day away. Kendall and Reign had too many things to do before the show to be gone more than one day and one night. They planned to drive back to the gallery as soon as their plane touched down the next day.

Their time in New York City flew by, but it was a very beneficial trip. Kendall and Reign stayed at Hotel Bossert. They made it to Trixie's apartment on time, met her, and had a tour around her studio. Kendall chose some pieces she liked, she and Trixie negotiated the terms of their future partnership, and then Trixie signed the Gallery 116 artist contract. Reign agreed after seeing Trixie's work that their customers would love what she had to offer.

The three of them dined at Colonie and then Kendall and Reign headed back to the hotel to make it an early night. This was meant to be a quick "meet Trixie" trip, not a "tour and shop and stay out late in New York City trip." They went to bed knowing that they had achieved what they flew to the city to do.

CHAPTER TEN

April 15–16

The month of March flew by. It was already April the 15th and the Gallery 116 Spring Art Show was the next night. The rental company was in the middle of dropping off cocktail tables, a banquet table, another small table for beverages, as well as several chairs and the florist was dropping off a few floral arrangements. All the gallery artists had dropped off their show pieces days ago, however Trixie Dixon, who was an official 116 artist now, had shipped all her pieces ahead of her own flight the next day. Kendall had several handymen assisting her and Reign in the picture hanging because for the show there were so many large pieces, and many of those large pieces needed complicated picture lights hung over them as well.

The gallery was a buzz of activity. The girls were in jeans and sweatshirts and sneakers. It was not a day to be concerned with high fashion. People were in and out of the gallery the entire day. And because of that, the girls had not stopped once for food.

At 3:15, Branton walked in the gallery door with a bag full of two 6-inch sub sandwiches, two bags of chips, a container of fruit, and two bottles of water.

Reign and Kendall both squealed with delight. They were ready for a break. Branton had given them the perfect excuse to stop for a bit. Immediately, they both sat down on the floor where they had been standing. Branton walked over and divided the food amongst the two of them. While he was at the gallery, he dropped off the name cards for his pieces, repaired a scratch on one of his frames, replaced a rubber bumper on the back of a frame that had fallen off in transit, and then asked the girls if there was anything else he could do.

Kendall said, "No, thank you, B. Actually, we are in good shape. Once the florist drops off the flowers a little bit later, I'm going to decorate all the cocktail tables, set out some of the serving pieces that the caterer will need for tomorrow, and then head to the store to purchase coffee and tea, lemonade, and champagne for the show. Our caterer is only responsible for food. When I get home, I am going to make a few calls to personally remind and invite people to the show. Please do the same, both of you. Branton, you and the other artists have created such beautiful pieces for the show, I want as many people as we can get here the first night as possible. I really do think it could be a record attendance night for us here at Gallery 116."

"I sure hope so," said Branton! "Trixie, alone, should bring in her own crowd now that everyone knows she is one of your artists."

"Yea!" Reign said enthusiastically. "She mentioned to us that she is a hot item and that many galleries had been pursuing her. We have gotten so many calls about her work since Kendall signed her. It will be nice to introduce her to our customers, so they can ask her questions in person. Hopefully, she is good at selling her own work. People love meeting the artist of a piece of art they plan to purchase. Isn't that right, Hon?"

"Apparently, they do. I'll be dressed in my tux for the event to impress all my favorite customers and all of my potential ones," Branton said winking at Kendall and Reign.

The group was then interrupted by the arrival of the florist. They assisted in helping her bring in the floral arrangements along with some extra flowers Kendall would be using as additional decorations. Branton left shortly after the florist, and then Reign and Kendall left right at closing time. They wanted to get plenty of rest and to save their energy for the next workday and for the show the next evening. Kendall decided to keep the gallery open during the day just for customers who were unable to make it during the evening show hours. She also was expecting certain designers to drop by during the day to get first dibs on paintings before Kendall began putting the red sold dots on the purchased pieces as she did during the show as her regular customers started buying. Kendall began her process of placing red dots on sold paintings as soon as the show started, and the designers always seemed to prefer choosing pieces during the less crowded afternoon hours on show days to avoid the show frenzy. Kendall appreciated her designers very much, so she wanted to make accommodations whenever needed and being open during those additional hours before a show seemed to be the solution and going home early helped her rest up for what was sure to be one busy day ahead.

Kendall was truly excited about the show this year. She felt she had the best selection she had ever had in the gallery. She certainly had a few pieces that had the highest prices she had ever charged for paintings. Her artists created pieces that were worthy of the prices and her customers were willing to pay. Placing those sold dots was going be thrilling, but she was ready to head home for the night. Kendall was a bit rushed leaving the gallery because she was hoping to make it back to her neighborhood in time to pick up her special dress at the dry cleaners before they closed.

Kendall pulled into the dry cleaners' parking lot at closing time. Luckily, she knew the owner, Mrs. Kim. She saw her sitting inside as Kendall tugged on the locked door. Thankfully, Mrs. Kim happily opened the door, so Kendall could pick up her dress. On the rest of her drive home she called Cait's parents, Tish, Madge, Mama and Harry to personally invite them to the gallery even though Kendall knew it was expecting a lot to ask them to get rides into the city to attend the show. Most of her customers lived in the city and would make a night of it, by grabbing dinner before attending. Many of her clients made big plans to attend. It was sure to be a formal evening affair for many. A photographer from the local newspaper was always assigned to attend and to take photos for the society page. And, these days, influencers were asked to attend by various city groups to post and promote the downtown activities and trend setting establishments like galleries and clubs. Kendall always enjoyed trying to spot those attendees. She could usually do so by noticing their choice of attire and noticing their age. They were always handsome or beautiful and seemed to get younger and younger year after year as Kendall got older and older.

The sun was shining through the bedroom window as Kendall first opened her eyes the next morning after a very good night's rest. She headed to the kitchen for a cup of coffee before anything else. Just as she finished adding the oat milk creamer to her coffee, Kendall could hear her cell phone buzzing on the table in the front hall next to her purse. Kendall grabbed her coffee mug and sped to answer her phone.

"Hello?" Kendall asked after not seeing the number as she hurriedly answered.

"Kendall, it is Mom. I know it is early and I don't want to bother you, but I know it is the 16th, and I remembered that your big show is tonight. I wanted to tell you that I hope it is a success and that you enjoy every minute selling all the paintings I know you are going to sell. I would normally not bother you and you know that, but I wanted you to know that I was thinking about you on this big day, and I wanted you to hear from me about how much I love you. Your dad and I are so proud of you. I hope you know we would be there for you if we could. I cannot wait to hug you next month when you get here. Can you believe it is only a few weeks away?"

"No, Mom, I cannot believe it! Thank you so much for calling me! It means a whole lot. Reign and I have put a lot of time and energy into this show and my artists are talented, so I just know the show will be a success. I cannot wait to see you too. Tell Dad I love and miss him too. Thanks so much for calling, Mom, but I have got to get in the shower so I can get to work. I have a few things to accomplish this morning so Reign and I can relax this afternoon and evening."

Kendall called Reign on the way to work hoping to catch her before she got to the gallery. "I need you to run to the bank to get us some cash for tonight. Most everyone will be paying with a card, but sometimes we do have cash purchases, and I do not want to be stuck without change," Kendall said.

"I can do that. Is there anything else we need before I come in?" Reign asked knowing that they would probably be running out all day for things they forgot.

"No, I think we are all set. Thanks so much, Reign! I cannot tell you how much your help is making this whole show possible. I could not do it this year, at least the way we are doing it *this* year, without you," Kendall said with much thankfulness. Kendall hung up the phone as she pulled up to the gallery. She got out of the car carrying a huge box filled with all the beverages for the evening. She finally had to put the cumbersome extra-heavy box down on the ground outside in order to open the door. She decided to leave it at the door and carry individual items into the kitchen. She placed the lemonade and the champagne in the refrigerator, so they would be chilled by party time. The coffee she would start brewing just before the crowd arrived, so she left it in the kitchen next to the coffee maker. Then, she placed the assorted teas near the teacups and the hot water carafe on the beverage table.

Kendall used the single orange Gerbera daisies the florist had brought for the vases on each cocktail table. She took a few moments to fill the vases with water and recut the stems before placing each stem in a vase. After Reign got back from the bank, she helped Kendall decide where to place the large floral arrangements. They opted to put one on the welcome desk and the largest one in the center of the food table. Kendall dug in her desk to find her red dots, brought in her dress and shoes from the car, chose the jazz and classical playlists to play during the show, and then headed to the airport to pick up Trixie Dixon. Reign was staying behind to be available for customers, artists or the caterers in case it took Kendall longer than expected at the airport.

Kendall sat in the cell phone lot for a few minutes because Trixie's plane had not landed yet. When it did land and after Trixie had retrieved her bag, Kendall picked her up at the curb to save time.

"How was the flight?" Kendall asked as Trixie jumped in the car after putting her bag in the trunk.

"Great and thanks for picking me up! I'm getting excited about tonight! I hope you received all my paintings in good shape."

"Oh Yes, we did! Did you not get my message? I called as soon as we uncrated them all. I love every single one you sent. They are going to do well tonight."

Trixie flippantly explained, "Oh I never check my messages, especially when I am working. I cannot wait to tour the gallery and see the set-up."

When they arrived back at the gallery, Kendall walked Trixie around pointing out and explaining the work of the other 116 artists. Kendall was thrilled with how the gallery looked decorated and ready for guests. They were just awaiting the caterers' food delivery.

Trixie questioned, "Why is my work placed all the way in the back of the gallery? I am the most well-known, you know?"

Kendall said trying to explain and defend herself, "Well my thinking was to have the artwork of the artists our customers are most familiar with up front. I wanted the customers to make their way to the back, passing all the familiar artwork as they make their way to see yours. We have so many planning to come see your pieces exclusively, that way they see everything else we have to offer while doing so."

Trixie said, "O.k. I guess I get it. Is there anywhere I can get away and sit down? It has been a long day for me already." Kendall walked her to the office where Reign was following up on some customer calls and printing the artists' statement and bio pages to have on hand for the show. Trixie annoyingly looked at Reign and said, "Well I was hoping to be alone, but I guess this will do. What time is the show anyway? I am wearing what I have on, so I don't need to get ready or anything."

Kendall said, "The show starts at six o'clock." As she said it, Kendall glanced past Trixie and caught Reign's eye. Reign made a quick face and rolled her eyes. Kendall hoped the evening would go off without a hitch having five artist personalities in the building at one time. Only time would tell. She then walked out of the office after hearing the bell at the front door. She assumed it was the arrival of the caterers.

Kendall greeted the caterers and helped hold the door open as they brought in all of the trays and platters of baked brie, roast beef mini sliders, crab dip with crackers, fruit, cheese, charcuterie, and especially mini tortes of assorted flavors which Kendall had requested because she wanted her guests to be able top the night off with a sweet bite. Looking at the trays pass by made Kendall's tummy roar. She had not stopped for food again today and had not eaten a thing since breakfast, and really, she could not even remember what she had eaten because she had eaten while on the phone with her mother. And she had been so shocked by the call, it wiped her memory.

Kendall walked back into the office after the caterers left. She whispered to Reign, "Go look at how spectacular the table looks." Kendall whispered because Trixie was now asleep on the floor with her head on her backpack. She was positioned in such a way that her cropped top revealed her various belly tattoos. Kendall stepped right over her to get to the computer on her desk so that she could quietly start playing the music she had selected to play during the show. Then, Kendall got up to change into her dress and reapply her makeup and put a few curls in her long brown hair.

Reign was shocked when Kendall emerged from the restroom a changed woman in her sleek skintight red satin dress, wearing a simple gold and pearl necklace, pearl earrings and with her hair curled and hanging loosely around her face. She was also wearing her red bottom black heels. Reign looked beautiful too in her gold knee-length cocktail dress with her blonde locks in a loose chignon with loose pieces to soften her face, but she knew she could not compete with Kendall. Tonight was Kendall's big night, and Reign thought Kendall looked and dressed like she was ready for it.

The first customers to enter the gallery after all the artists had arrived weren't customers, but her neighbors. Tish was the driver that drove Mama, Madge, Peg, Larry and Harry in her Suburban all the way into the city so they could support Kendall and her gallery. Harry whistled as he walked in and spotted Kendall.

Kendall turned around to spot the group walking in the door. Her heart was so full, and her eyes filled with tears as she invited them in, gave them each a hug, and thanked them for making the effort. It meant the world to her.

"We can't stay long. We need to get back before it gets too dark, but show us all around," said Tish. Madge made a beeline to the food table and Mama complimented Kendall on her lovely dress. Harry said, "Introduce me to the artist of the painting you gave me, please. I've got questions for him."

Kendall walked Harry over to where Branton was visiting with a group of customers. It was 6:15 and the gallery was already full to the brim. Susie and Leslie and Inglewood were congregating around the food table. Trixie sleepily walked out of the office in her black jeans, cropped concert t-shirt and her combat boots. Kendall could see she was finally making her way to the back of the gallery. Reign walked up to Kendall asking where Branton was. "I just left him all dressed up in his tux chatting with Harry. Is he not still with him?" Kendall said looking around the gallery. In her heels she was a bit taller than Reign. "I see him back there chatting with Trixie," Kendall said pointing.

Tish, Madge, Peg, Larry and Harry approached Kendall complimenting her on the food choices. "Everything is delicious," said Madge.

Kendall said, "That was all Reign and the caterers. She helped me choose the best in the business for tonight."

One of Kendall's favorite customers pulled her aside to say he wanted to purchase Susie's largest piece. So, Kendall took her first red dot and placed it on that painting's tag.

While walking back to the back of the gallery, Reign could hear lots of laughter and giggling. As she got closer, she realized it was Branton and Trixie. They seemed to be having a jolly 'ole time. As she approached them Branton said, "You have to hear this story, Hon. Trixie just finished telling me the story behind her latest piece." Reign looked directly at Trixie and said, "Well then, do tell."

Back at the front door, Kendall was welcoming all her guests. At seven on the dot, in the door walked Anthony with a group of guy friends. She was floored when she saw him arrive. He walked directly over to her, kissed her on her cheek, introduced her to his friends, congratulated her on a busy show, and then asked if his mom was still there.

Kendall said, "Yes. In fact, she is. I was so shocked to see so many of my neighbors here. Does she know you are coming?"

"No, she told me she was coming on the phone this morning, but I kept my plan a secret. I wanted to surprise them all."

Just before he left her to connect with his mom, he looked her directly in the eyes and told her how beautiful she looked. Kendall got weak in the knees, and it wasn't because she was tired from a busy day. She watched him walk away in his navy pinstripe suit. He was still the most handsome man she had ever seen.

The evening continued with purchase after purchase. Anthony ended up meeting and purchasing one of Leslie's large abstracts in blues and oranges, of course. He said he had been looking for months for something similar. Branton sold all ten of his pieces. Inglewood sold three of his portraits and had three individuals commission him for portraits. Susie, of course, sold *all* her pieces. And, Trixie had lots of interest in her paintings too. Many of Kendall's customers were excited to see Kendall representing Trixie's work. They had heard great things about it all, but it was going to take them time to be sold on it. It helped to know the stories behind each piece in a style like Trixie's. Trixie was depending on Kendall to sell her pieces, and it was hard for Kendall to stay with her all night. Kendall was being pulled by one artist or another all night, not to mention the customers and designers. Branton, on the other hand, had spent the entire night back in Trixie's section, but his works sold themselves.

Her neighbors left around 7:30. Kendall was so thrilled they had come out. Mama had loved seeing Anthony all dressed up and out with his friends. As they all left, they hugged Kendall's neck and reminded her to stop by their homes for visits in her free time. They had all come to adore her.

After they left, Anthony stood talking to Kendall for a bit about his painting purchase and his plan for where he was going to hang it in his loft. He asked her if she might be interested in grabbing dinner after work one night in the coming weeks. She assured him that she would be thrilled to join him. She let him know, in no uncertain terms, that she was interested in dinner and him. It had been months since Colin broke things off with her, and she realized that she was ready to take a chance on love again.

Reign came storming through the gallery looking furious and asking for Kendall's help with the card scanner which did not seem to be working. Kendall excused herself and followed Reign to the front counter. She had not seen Reign angry ever, so she was confused.

"What has you in a tizzy? Is it really the card machine? We do have a backup in the office if that is the case."

"No, it isn't the machine! Have you seen dapper Branton all decked out in his tux? Nope, I bet you haven't! He has been in the back of the gallery *with Trixie* ALL night."

"I would not take it too seriously. Branton is a friendly guy, and she is another artist—a kindred spirit. Don't let it ruin your night. Go grab some food and come back here. I'll introduce you to Anthony."

"I will. I want to meet him before he heads out. But Trixie is our age, and she is beautiful! I can see it underneath her tough artist act."

Kendall said, "Reign, she may be 28, but age does not mean maturity. We know that. She thinks she is big time. Let her have her moment. Branton will be by your side by the end of the night. I know him. He's a bit of a flirt, but I know he is serious about you."

Kendall introduced Reign to Anthony, and she was quite impressed. Reign thought he seemed perfect for Kendall. Reign knew Kendall had told her he was an architect, but she had forgotten. They chatted about design for quite a while.

Kendall and Reign both enjoyed meeting the friends Anthony brought along with him too. He had some good, solid friends that were not bad looking either. Branton noticed their group chatting in a circle from across the room. He did not love seeing Reign smiling and chuckling with Kendall and all the other guys, so he made his way to stand by Reign's side just as Anthony and his friends were leaving, just as Kendall said he would. He put his arm around Reign's waist and whispered, "I am so sorry I left you alone for most of the evening."

At just before nine, a group of influencers walked through the door, each carrying a phone and heading straight for the champagne. A few minutes later they could be seen taking selfies with each artist and in front of some of the main show pieces, mostly the ones with red dots. They were not there to purchase; they were there to see and be seen and record the event to post to social media later in the evening. Kendall did not mind. She expected it, and it was all free advertising.

By 10, the party had begun winding down. One last customer, Mr. Jack Peterson, was making the last purchase. The total for the evening was somewhere around one hundred thousand and that did not even include the commissioned pieces that were ordered or Trixie's paintings that customers were considering. It had been a very successful evening. As the last customer exited the gallery, Kendall raised her glass and her voice too saying, "I want to thank each and every one of you for making the night such a success. To Branton, Leslie, Inglewood, Susie and Trixie, thanks for sharing your creations with us. And thank you for working so hard to provide the pieces that you did. To Reign, you have been a life saver to me for months. Thanks for putting in the hard work. I'd say it paid off. Now, I'm going to turn off the music, everyone grab some food to take with you. Let's call it a night. We will clean everything up tomorrow. Artists, keep painting! It doesn't stop here! This was only a public introduction. We will need your best work like never before after tonight. I cannot wait to read the reviews in the morning!" With that, everyone grabbed their things and Kendall headed out to drop Trixie at her hotel. Reign and Branton were the last to leave because Branton had continued to apologize and to explain why he was hanging with Trixie all night to try to make things right with Reign.

Kendall woke up to her inbox full of emails with links to her show reviews. Every single one of the reviews she received was positive and glowing. Each one mentioned Kendall's hard work and giftedness in choosing artists to represent, as well as her knack for knowing what pieces to choose to show that highlight the best work of each selected artist. There were reviews of all her artists too, along with an introduction to Trixie's work which would bring future clients to the gallery. Even though her shows are one-night events, the reviews always encourage those interested to stop by during normal business hours because the unsold pieces hang for weeks to months after a show ends. Branton got a glowing review in the local paper as well. It was a normal occurrence for him, but Kendall knew Branton and Reign would both still be excited to read about it, so she forwarded the email to both of them.

CHAPTER ELEVEN

May

Kendall could not believe that it was already May. She had one more task to complete on *the list*, and she was finally going to be able to cross that task off that list in two days when she was due to fly to Phoenix to visit her parents. She and Reign had finalized all of the numbers from the show. They had a record attendance and record sales. Three customers came through and purchased three of Trixie's pieces. Kendall had finally contacted Trixie to let her know. Although Trixie was still a bit sore about not selling out the first night, she was indeed happy that Kendall and Reign had completed three big sales since the night of the show. Kendall thought that the positive show reviews may have prompted buyers to decide to purchase Trixie's work. Trixie had an easily-offended personality along with a hard to please attitude, but Kendall was learning how to deal with it. Other than the fact that she flirted a bit too much with Branton, overall, Reign and Kendall still considered their decision to bring her on as a new artist the right thing to do and a wise decision. Their work was selling art and that is what they chose to focus on, especially since Trixie lived all the way in New York and they weren't going to see her every day. And Kendall had added a new artist to her number of artists which was another item crossed off *the list*.

Kendall and Reign considered the show a complete success, and it would certainly help them out with their numbers for the year, but they were on to other activities with their sights set on the summer and the fall. Kendall was already working with some new designers with a totally new group of clients that needed big important pieces and they were already making their plans to attend Art Basel in Miami in December. Kendall's calendar was filling up with more appointments and meetings than she knew what to do with. She had just been complaining to Reign about getting too busy again. She had not even had extra time after work to have dinner with Anthony or to stop by her neighbors for visits like they had asked. "Free time"—she was losing sight of what that phrase even meant. And Anthony had called to try to schedule something two times in the last two weeks, and they still could not find a time that worked for the both of them. She did not like the feeling of overwhelm that she was starting to feel. Reign did understand because getting together with Branton had been difficult for her since the show, and he had not been stopping by the gallery as much either. He said that he was focusing on painting, and Reign wanted to believe him because she had forgiven him for the Trixie situation at the show and she was still completely smitten with him.

Kendall had an appointment with a new designer at the gallery just before one. She had come highly recommended by Anthony. Anthony had worked with her on some recent commercial jobs, and she was looking for a connection to some inexpensive abstracts to be used in several large commercial office buildings downtown. Kendall was looking forward to the appointment before heading out of town for a week. Kendall ran to the restroom just before her appointment. Reign had to answer the phone just as Kendall left the office.

"Hello. Gallery 116, may I help you? This is Reign speaking."

"Reign," said a shaky but very distinguished voice. "This is Kendall's father. Is she in? May I speak with her? It is an emergency, and I need to talk with her ASAP." Reign held her hand over the receiver and yelled for Kendall who was in the back hall just outside the office.

"Who is it, Reign? I am right here."

"It is your father," Reign said handing Kendall the phone as she walked into the office.

"Dad, how are you? Why are you calling me on the gallery phone and not my cell? Is everything alright? You know I'm going to be there in two days. Is there something you and Mom want me to bring you?"

Reign looked over at Kendall as Kendall turned white as a ghost and gasped. Reign could hear that Kendall's father was still talking.

"Nooooooooo. You have got to be mistaken! Are you sure? I was going to see you both in two days. She didn't! She can't! Dad, nooooooooooo. It can't be true! Kendall began to sob, and she turned around and immediately threw up in her office trash can and fell over into her desk chair. Reign ran over to Kendall to feel her head and check her pulse. She grabbed the phone from Kendall, and asked if Kendall could call her father back in a bit. She was worried about Kendall, and she could not imagine what her dad had told her.

"Ken, what did he say?"

"He told me that my mom died this morning. She had a stroke just after breakfast and was gone before the ambulance could arrive. She apparently didn't suffer though." Reign hugged Kendall as she continued to sob. She sobbed. She sighed. She cried a lot. And she threw up again.

"What am I going to do now? I was planning to visit her. I would have seen her in two days. Now, when I go, she won't be there. I will never see her again." She choked a bit and coughed and coughed and sobbed some more. What would she do now? How could she be there for her father without her mother? How was she going to be able to comfort him alone? How could she live in a world without her mother?

As Reign heard someone enter the gallery she turned to Kendall and said, "You stay and call your father back. I will talk to your next appointment. I will meet with her and let her know what happened and see how I can help her with what she needs. I've got you covered, Ken." Kendall got up, walked to the bathroom to splash cold water on her face, took a few deep breaths, and then called her father back to discuss things in a more mature and controlled manner. She needed details and she had to talk to her father to get them.

After her meeting with the designer, Reign walked back to the office with a Sprite on ice for Kendall only to find Kendall with her head on her desk crying silently and sniffing with every breath.

Reign persuaded Kendall to go home for the rest of the day. Reign offered to drive her home, but Kendall felt confident that she could make it on her own. Kendall let Reign know that she would still be heading to Phoenix the day after tomorrow, but she would probably need to stay longer than she had initially planned.

Reign said, "You know I will handle things here for you. You do not need to worry about that at all. I am sure I can get Branton to move his studio to the gallery for a bit just to have a second person here for the time being because he has no trips planned anytime soon. He knows the art and artist side as much or more than I do. I know he will want to help you out with whatever you need. You go home, see Fendy, and get some rest. I have got it covered here."

Kendall drove the whole way home with tear blurred vision while listening to the song "Mother Like Mine" by The Band Perry. By the time she pulled into the carport, Kendall felt like she had been crushed by a ton of bricks. She had cried her daily allotment of tears and as a result, all the energy she had left was used to put one foot in front of the other just so she could make it safely into the house. Fendy met Kendall at the door meowing in what sounded like complete sentences while weaving between Kendall's legs offering comfort in the only way she could. Just as Kendall placed her purse and phone on the front entry table, she heard a soft knock at the door. She had no idea who it might be.

As Kendall opened the door, Mama Leone blew passed her right through the front door and walked into Kendall's living room and then immediately into the kitchen. "Oh my, sweet Kendall! Anthony called and told me what happened. I am so sorry!" Mama said after emptying her armload full of casserole dishes onto the counter. Then she ran to give Kendall the biggest bear hug saying, "Now I have brought you some lasagna, some of Tish's bread, and an antipasto salad. I will start some hot tea for you. Now, you go sit down, put your feet up, and rest. I'm here for you for the rest of the night. I'll warm the food up. I can start you a bath if you would like. I am here if you want to chat or not if you want to just be quiet, but I will not leave you alone."

Kendall could not believe her thoughtfulness and kindness, but she just had to ask, "How in the world did Anthony even know?"

"Well, you had that appointment with that designer that had worked with Anthony before. She apparently heard from Reign at the appointment. And she called Anthony to inform him as soon as she heard. She assumed Anthony would want to know. Anthony called me because he knew you would head home eventually, and he knows we know what you are going through. He knows what it is like to lose someone near and dear and what that loss can do to a person. He did not want you experiencing that alone tonight, and I agreed. So, here I am. Don't be mad at Anthony. I think he already has a bit of a soft spot for you, and he tells me you two have been unsuccessful in finding a moment to have a meal together. Now, tonight isn't the night to get into it. And I am not trying to push you into a relationship with my Anthony, even though he is a great boy. But you kids have got to make a little more room in your schedules for life. If not, it will make the room for you, like it did in yours today."

"I know!" Kendall said crying again. "If I had not been so busy with the gallery, I would have already visited my parents before today. I would have gotten to see and hug my mom one last time. I am so mad at myself for getting so caught up in being successful and making a living. I have not visited my parents in two years, and I was just *two* days away from a flight to Phoenix. I do not know how I am going to forgive myself or how I'm going to get over this."

"Well, for one thing, dying is part of living. It is bound to happen to those we love the most. It happened to me and Anthony. We know the pain of loss. It hurts. But blaming yourself for making a living at your age is nothing to be ashamed of. You have worked hard from what I can see. You have a great gallery and a successful career. That is a good thing. Only you know if your priorities were askew. You cannot live in the past. What is done is done. Get your priorities straight *now*. *Now* is what counts. Your mother would want you to be happy, for you to find your happiest happy surrounded by friends and family that love you. Make that a goal, rather than being angry at yourself for what you woulda, coulda, shoulda done."

Kendall said, "Thank you for the great food, wisdom and company, Mama. I really appreciate it, but I need a bit of distraction. Want to watch a cooking show?"

"Do I want to watch a cooking show? You better bet I do! I just wish I had brought my notebook!" They sat watching shows for at least an hour. By the end of the second show, Kendall was starting to feel a tad bit better. Anthony called on his mom's phone and asked to speak to Kendall.

"Kendall, I am so sorry to hear about your mother. I hope my mom has brought you some comfort and company this evening. I hated for you to spend the evening all alone. I sure hope you don't mind that I shared the news with her. She thinks her cooking heals anything, and it usually does. Thanks for opening your door for her. I'm sure you did her as much good as she did you. You will be in my thoughts and prayers while you are in Phoenix. And remember, you still owe me a dinner when you return!"

"Thanks so much, Anthony, for checking in and for sending your mom over as well. Yes, we must get dinner when I get back. I'll hold you to it. Keep in touch!"

As soon as Kendall got off the phone with Anthony, Mama said that it was getting late so she thought she just might better head home to bed if Kendall thought she could be alone and still fall off to sleep. Kendall assured her that she would be alright. Kendall hugged her, thanked her and walked her to the door just as Kendall's cell phone started ringing.

Mama said, "You run get that! Have a good night's sleep and a safe trip! Call me tomorrow if you don't go into work and need more company."

Kendall quickly answered her phone. It was her father checking on her before she went to bed.

"Kendall, I am calling just to see how you made it the rest of the day. I wanted to share a few things before you went to sleep tonight. Just know a day never went by when your mom did not mention you. You were her pride and joy. She was always so proud of you. She often told me that once you left the nest and hit the big time that you wouldn't be back. She knew we couldn't compete with that world. She loved you, Kendall, with all she had, just know that. She had hoped that you would find someone more suited for you and our family other than Colin. Just know that I will continue to pray that you find that special someone that loves you for you like we always have and the way I loved your mother. I wanted you to hear all of that tonight, and I wanted to tell you how much I love you and how proud I am of you before you went to sleep. Darling, I know it has been a tough day for us both. I can't wait to see you the day after tomorrow. I will be at the airport to pick you up with a pep in my step. I hate that it is under these circumstances, but I'm looking forward to laying my eyes on you, Dear One."

Kendall spent the next day in bed resting most of the day. She eventually got out of bed to repack her suitcase for Phoenix because she was going to need more things than she initially thought when she had excitedly packed a few days early.

Peg brought over her vegetable cheese soup and a plate of brownies when she visited to offer her condolences. And Harry kindly called to check on Kendall. He was another one of her sweet new friends who knew what she must be going through, and he wanted to personally check in to see if she was o.k.

It was the early evening when Kendall invited Mama over to watch television again and to share Peg's goodies, so they would not go to waste since she was leaving the next day. Kendall knew the company would be another needed distraction.

Kendall made it to Phoenix and made it through stepping into her parents' home for the first time in two whole years without her mom to greet her at the door. It stung. It hurt, but Kendall survived. She also survived the memorial service. It was hard for Kendall because she did not grow up in Phoenix and she had not visited there very often, so she did not know the people at the service. Many of her mother's friends did speak to Kendall about her mother. Her mother was indeed loved by those who knew her. Her parents moved out to Phoenix just a few years before they both retired, so Kendall's mom was not a teacher there very long. However, many of her former students and their parents attended and shared the impact that her mother made in their lives or in the lives of their children. Kendall was thankful that others had known and loved her mother as she had.

Kendall's father was doing well, considering. Her parents' friends were doing a great job surrounding him with comfort and love and companionship. During Kendall's visit, her parents' house had been full of food, so Kendall and her father did not have to worry about cooking, which was helpful and very nice for them both. Kendall had helped her father with estate paperwork and with going through her mother's things. It was a hard time, but she and her father had enjoyed reconnecting. That was the bright side of what they were going through.

Mama, Anthony, Reign and Branton had all been in constant contact with Kendall via calls and texts. They all wanted her to know she was on their minds.

Branton and Reign had the gallery under control. The customers loved being able to get a glimpse at Branton painting on location and between the two of them, they had closed several big sales which Kendall was thankful for.

Kendall had enjoyed spending time at her mother and father's house. It had brought back lots of old memories. In the cleaning out and organizing, Kendall found her old yearbooks, some old school artwork and papers, her first pair of shoes, a lock of hair from her first haircut, her first dolls, lots of drawings and other artwork, and lots of old pictures and photo albums. She even found some of her old baby clothes and blankets that were in very good shape. She was indeed an only child and her mom had cherished every moment and had kept and saved *everything*.

Kendall's father had been an accountant before retiring. Kendall had talked with her father about starting to volunteer to help people with their taxes. She thought it could give him something to do that could really help others and that would get him out of the house and around other people.

Kendall had plans to stay until the end of the month to get everything with her father squared away and in good order. She wanted to help him do everything that needed doing to ensure that he could not just survive, but thrive on his own, especially with her so far away. And she felt things at home were as good as could be expected. Mama was checking in on Fendy daily. They were apparently forming quite a bond and with a cat like Fendy, that was saying something.

CHAPTER TWELVE

June

Kendall was finally back in town. She had taken a few days to stay at home, to relax and to visit with the neighbors. Branton was back in his own studio, and Reign was adjusting to having her best girlfriend by her side again every day while also adjusting to Branton not being by her side every moment of every day. The previous month had been great for their relationship, however. Their time together was not too much, and it did them good. Surprisingly, they worked very well together. Reign had especially enjoyed watching Branton paint during the times when they did not have customers in the gallery.

June had always been a slow month for the gallery in years past. And this year was proving no different. So many of their customers traveled in June and July, but July was busier than June in the city because of the tourism in the area.

However, in her neighborhood, *June* was *the* big month because of the neighborhood block party. Kendall had never attended, nor had she ever even been at home during one, but apparently each year the neighbors block off all of Hanover Lane and set up chairs and tables all down the street. Mama and Peg and Larry and Harry had told her all about it because it usually turned out to be the highlight of their summer. This year it was planned for the first Saturday in June, which was the next Saturday. Kendall was planning on attending and she was glad she would not be having to take the day off since the gallery was closed every Saturday during the summer.

This was going to be a big June week for her not only because of the block party, but because she and Anthony had finally nailed down time to have dinner. He asked her to go to dinner on Friday night. They were meeting after work at Billings Bistro. It was supposed to be a brand-new quaint restaurant with an up-and-coming top-notch chef. She and Anthony were both excited to try it and were looking forward to getting together. Between now and then, she had to come up with a recipe for homemade ice cream, however. Kendall had been chosen to be one of the ice cream contributors for the block party. She thought the ice cream would be something she could whip up easily on Saturday morning if she had a recipe and the supplies on standby. She did have her own ice cream maker. It was one of the things her parents had given her as a housewarming present, that and a fondue set, both things she had grown up using with her parents. She would check when she got home, but she thought she just might have a family recipe in the ice cream freezer box. "Homemade vanilla" ice cream, specifically, had always been her favorite ice cream flavor. She chose to make it for that reason and because vanilla ice cream seemed to be a safe choice for a crowd. Kendall was providing a variety of toppings to please the neighbors who do not love plain vanilla by allowing them to create their own more exciting custom flavors. She felt that it was the least she could do to make up for such a basic summer party contribution.

It was already Tuesday. She was leaving a bit early to get home in time to take Fendy to the vet for her yearly shots. Fendy was not a fan, therefore neither was Kendall. The whole ordeal put them both in a tizzy every year. Fendy wasn't much up for crates *or* car rides. Colin had taken Fendy the last few years, so Kendall was gearing up for the appointment to be a responsible pet owner proving to Colin and to the world that she could, in fact, do hard things.

The trip to the vet went better than expected. In fact, it made her want to call and brag to Colin, but she didn't dare. The vet did give Kendall a bit of a guilt trip about Fendy's weight though. Kendall tried to explain Fendy's feeding schedule and serving amount along with the fact that someone else had been feeding Fendy for Kendall for the last month while she had been in Phoenix. She wasn't quite sure if the vet believed her story or not. She certainly did not *seem* to believe her. Kendall knew that Mama must believe the same about cat food as she did about her own cooking--that it has healing properties. Kendall would not be surprised if Mama had given Fendy a nightly serving of her special pasta sauce and a serving of Tiramisu to go along with her kitty chow. Mama apparently spoiled her rotten or at least spoiled her up four pounds. She would not dare mention anything about the weight gain to Mama because Kendall was thankful Mama had tended to Fendy and because Mama and Fendy had become such fast friends. Kendall *now* knew the way Mama must have worked her way into Fendy's heart--through her little cat tummy.

Friday arrived before Kendall could believe it. Kendall wore regular work clothes to work at the gallery all day, but she brought in a blue jumpsuit to change into for dinner. Reign had been teasing her all day about being nervous. Kendall wasn't really all that nervous because, by this point, Kendall and Anthony had seen each other on several casual occasions and chatted on the phone multiple times. It was certainly not a *blind* date. Anthony felt like a good friend by now, a rather good-looking good friend at that. Kendall liked his gentle, caring nature. He was a nice, respectable "Mama's boy" literally. He worked diligently at his architectural firm. He was successful with many important clients both in the city and around the area. He worked with both individual/private and commercial/corporate clients. Kendall loved his dry sense of humor. She always got his jokes and giggled accordingly, which he appreciated. Apparently, that wasn't always the case. His humor was smart and witty, and Kendall was smart and witty too, so they just worked well together.

Kendall also loved and appreciated Anthony's sense of style. Kendall wondered if Reign had noticed his style too because Reign had made several comments about it the last several months, and Reign had only seen Anthony in person twice. Kendall assumed Reign just might be a little jealous because Reign was dating a not so starving artist who was handsome, yes, but who loved his favorite painting overalls *maybe* a *bit too much* for Reign's taste.

Kendall changed into a blueprint blue jumpsuit chosen only to impress Anthony, the architect. She curled her hair and then twirled it into an updo allowing a few loose pieces of hair to fall softly around her face, then slipped on her heels and checked her reflection in the full-length mirror, added a touch of sparkling pink lip gloss and exited the restroom. Reign thought Kendall looked beautiful and stunning in her classic evening dinner look as she walked into the office. Reign knew that Kendall was going to blow Anthony's socks off because although Kendall's favorite color was green, the choice to wear blue was the perfect detail Anthony was sure to adore.

And she was right. Anthony turned bright red and started sweating a bit the minute he saw her enter the restaurant. Kendall was the most beautiful woman he had ever laid eyes on. He thought that that first night when he ran into her at Mulligan's and again at her gallery show. Seeing her again did not dull his feelings because he knew she was just as beautiful inside as she was on the outside. He had really gotten to know her with all their phone chats lately. Mama had also talked all about her to him which gave him more insight into who she truly was.

Anthony and Kendall each ordered corn and crab chowder, the salmon special with mashed potatoes and seasonal vegetables, and Anthony ordered a bottle of wine for the table. They split a warm maple blondie with caramel sauce and pretzel crumbles with maple ice cream for dessert. Their conversation flowed naturally the entire night. There was never a lull in conversation. They laughed and giggled, conversed and challenged each other. They were both sad when the night was over. As they were leaving the restaurant, it began to rain, but they did not care. It was Friday night, they were both heading straight home afterward, and they were just so thankful to finally spend an evening alone together. They stood in the rain chatting when Anthony leaned over and gave Kendall the kiss of a lifetime, at least that was how she described it to Reign on their phone call on her way home.

After Anthony's kiss, Kendall looked him in the eyes again and told him that she *really* wanted to see him again *real* soon. "Like tomorrow," she said. "We are having the neighborhood block party tomorrow. You should come!"

"I have already been planning to go. Mama asked me to attend. I think she wants me there because she knows you are going to be there this year, and she thinks we are too busy to have dinner. Little does she know that that is exactly what we just did. I cannot wait to tell her when I see her tomorrow. She will be stunned."

"I cannot wait to see you then! I must introduce you to Fendy and to show you around my little house in the suburbs."

"I cannot wait to see it. I will be bringing my dog too. Hopefully that will not disturb anyone at the party."

"Oh Anthony, you can do no wrong! You have my neighbors wrapped around your finger. They adore you. We must get going. I am drenched." Anthony kissed her one more time before grabbing her hand and quickly walking her to her car.

"You have a safe trip back to the burbs. Thank you so much for a fantastic night. I am glad we finally made it work. See you tomorrow, Beautiful!" Anthony said before walking back to his own car in the pouring rain. He did not mind one bit because he had had one heck of a night. He was already starting to fall hard for Kendall. She was just the girl to make him want to open his heart again. He had already decided that she was worth the risk.

Kendall drove away thinking about how Anthony was working his way into her heart, even though they had just had their *first* date. After that date, she could just tell that there was *finally room* in her heart to love another. She could feel the open space and she thought that Anthony might just be the one to fill it.

Kendall got up early the next morning to start the ice cream after her morning coffee. First, she drank her coffee while daydreaming about what a wonderful night she had had with Anthony the night before. She thought it was funny that for once she knew a boy's mother almost as well as she knew the boy she was dating. She would be seeing that boy and his mom again in a few short hours. Kendall was super excited for the day ahead. She was looking forward to seeing all her neighbors together now that it was warm weather, and of course she was excited to see Anthony and his dog in her very own neighborhood. "Life has a funny way of coming together sometimes," she thought to herself. Her mother would have approved of Anthony. She was certain of it. He might just be the answer to her mother's prayers, or her mother's and father's prayers.

Kendall got out all the ingredients she would need to make her vanilla ice cream recipe. She was using the family recipe that had indeed been inside the freezer box where she thought it might be.

Kendall began by cooking the custard on the stove, then she folded in the egg whites and then put it all into the chilled freezer container and then placed it in the refrigerator to chill a bit before starting the freezer just before the party started.

After she completed the first phase of the ice cream making process and cleaned up the kitchen, she fed Fendy and then jumped into the shower to make herself presentable for the day.

Kendall dressed in cutoff jean shorts, a green t-shirt and sneakers. It was a casual affair that was certain to be toasty by party time. After getting dressed Kendall headed outside to assist with the set-up. As soon as she appeared in her yard, Harry waved at her to join him near the designated food table.

"Howdy, Sweet Girl! I have not seen you for a bit. How are you? How was your time in Phoenix with your father? Did you help him handle things? Hey, do you mind walking back with me to the house to help me carry my contributions for today."

"Certainly, I would be glad to! My time with my father was good. We were able to accomplish a lot during my time there. How have you been?" Kendall said, putting an arm around Harry and walking to his house.

Once inside Harry started chatting. "I have been wanting to let you know that Cora finally reached out to me. Apparently, she is pregnant, and it finally dawned on her that she still needed her parents. When she called, I had to break it to her that Mildred was no longer with us. That truly broke her heart, and it did mine again. We talked about a lot of things. She apologized for never apologizing about her decisions, the ones she made independently. She has always blamed us for her decisions, but she didn't this time. She is even coming for a visit soon. Oh, and I forgot to tell you I contacted your friend Hilda a while back. She has been helping me out some. She helped me make this cheese and fruit platter for today, which we need to take out to the table. I invited her to the party today too, so she will be joining us," Harry said grabbing all the "soda pop" (that is what he preferred to call it) he was supplying, as well.

As the two of them headed outside Kendall said, "Harry I am so happy for you! Please let me know when Cora is in town. I would love to meet her! She has a very special father, so I am sure she is lovely. And I want to congratulate you on becoming a future grandpa. And I cannot wait to see Hilda today. I am so happy she has been able to help you out, and that she has been able to stay and work in the neighborhood."

Kendall dropped off the cheese platter and ran inside her house to start the ice cream freezer. It required some supervision, so she remained inside in her kitchen tending to it until the party started.

Kendall started the machine and covered it with bagged ice and rock salt sitting on the counter while scrolling through her phone and waiting for the yumminess to be ready for consumption.

She was focused on checking her social media and the freezer was quite noisy, but she thought she heard a slight knock at the door. She wasn't sure, so she didn't move from the counter. The next thing she saw was the most gorgeous Irish Setter bounding into her kitchen sniffing and wagging its tail. Kendall squealed, frightened and confused.

Anthony could be heard yelling, "Kendall! Kendall! Cola where are you, girl?", from Kendall's front room.

Kendall replied yelling from the kitchen. "Anthony, is that you? Holy cow! Is this your dog? It scared me to death. I could not hear anything. I'm in the kitchen working on freezing the ice cream." Then she quickly jumped off the counter and met Anthony in her front room.

"I am sorry for walking in on you. Mama told me you were in here and to walk on in if you did not answer which, now that I think of it, wasn't sound advice. This is my dog, Cola, and she is a girl. Sorry you two met that way."

"Oh, no worries. I am glad to get to meet her," Kendall said bending down to get in Cola's face and to rub her ears. "She's a beauty! Nice to see you, Anthony! Come on back to the kitchen for a sec, and then I will take you on a quick tour around my humble abode before we head out to join in the festivities. I may leave the ice cream inside after it is finished until dessert time, so it does not melt too much out in the heat."

She walked back over to give him a kiss and to let him know how happy she was to have him in the suburbs and inside her very own house, finally.

After Kendall gave Anthony the tour and introduced him and Cola to Fendy, they headed outside to congregate with the neighbors. All the ladies of the neighborhood loved Anthony, so they swarmed around him as soon as they saw him. Kendall chatted with Peg and Larry and Hilda and Harry and met many others she did not know. It turned out to be a delightful day. Cola behaved and the ladies eventually gave Anthony and Kendall time to themselves to chat. Anthony shared lots of memories of growing up in the neighborhood with all the kids of the people in attendance. And Kendall's homemade plain vanilla ice cream was a big hit without all the toppings and add-ins she supplied. Everyone that tried it was hooked after the first taste just as she had told them they would be. She may have even converted some lifetime chocolate ice cream lovers in the process.

When the party was over and when everything was cleaned up and when the street was reopened, Kendall joined Mama and Anthony at Mama's house for a light dinner and some watching of cooking shows. It was fun just the three of them, and Cola of course. Mama had tried to persuade Kendall to bring over Fendy too. Kendall had to explain that she wasn't *that* kind of cat. Truth be told, she wanted Mama and Anthony to herself without that added responsibility. Mama was thrilled anyway to have her darling Anthony and Kendall, both at her house. That was the kind of thing that made Mama's heart sing these days.

While the three were sitting down to dinner, they could hear a lawn mower outside. Kendall asked, "Who in the world could be mowing at this hour, especially in this neighborhood after such a busy afternoon?"

Mama explained, "It is probably Madge. She mentioned that she was so embarrassed that she had not mowed her yard and the one next door before the party today. She also hates to sweat too much doing it, so she usually waits until evenings to mow. Kendall, Madge is lovely, but she is a bit of a strange bird after losing her husband. She promised the Presleys before they moved that she would include their yard in her weekly yardwork schedule. She feels the need to help them since they have already moved out of state. I think it is too much work for her. Their house isn't even on the market, and she is far too old to mow two yards every week. At least I think so."

"Anthony, can you go out there to help her? I feel terrible for her," said Kendall.

"Just walk to the window and look out, Kendall. See if you think Anthony would actually be able to help if you can even *see* in the twilight outside. If you can see, you will notice that Madge mows in her housecoat. She stuffs her pockets full of her valuables while she does it so that no one steals anything from the house while she's out in the yard. She also yells cuss words while she pushes the mower. She has done this every summer for years, Hon. I do not think Anthony could help a thing. But he can certainly go try. It would be the kind thing to do, for sure."

Anthony came back in after being at Madge's for thirty minutes. She had let him mow only three strips of her own yard. "She was thankful and kind as usual." Anthony said, "She did tell me that the Presleys are finally putting their house on the market next month."

When Mama headed to bed, Anthony was not quite ready to head back into the city, so he and Cola and Kendall headed back to Kendall's house to watch one of her favorite movies, *Local Color*.

Once inside Kendall's house, Anthony felt like he needed to share the story of the loss of his last serious girlfriend with Kendall just to get it off his chest. She could not change anything, and it did not affect them directly now, but he felt that it was a part of his story that made him who he is, and he wanted to share it with her. They were alone, and it seemed like the right time.

It broke Kendall's heart to hear Anthony share the story, especially how it had changed him then like his own father's death had and how losing his girlfriend sometimes *still* affects him to this day. She could understand, in a way, because the situation over the holidays with Colin had her cautious about starting a new relationship, as well. Experiencing fear after a loss was something they both knew something about.

"I am so sorry that happened to you! That must have been rough on you so soon after losing your father."

"It was! I just wanted to tell you the story so if I seem cautious with you, that is why. I am really starting to fall for you. I think you are such a special girl. I think there really is something undeniable between us, and I do not want to mess up whatever it is. I don't want to lose you. I want to do whatever I need to do to keep you in my life. You are worth making this work."

"I agree, and I do not want to mess this up either," Kendall said leaning over to give Anthony another kiss as Cola nuzzled her way between the two wagging her tail and whimpering.

Anthony carefully pushed Cola away saying, "She might have some adjusting to do. It has been just me and Cola for quite a while now. She can be a jealous dog."

"Don't feel bad, Cola, Fendy is the same way. Ya'll can adjust together because we are both here to stay," said Kendall rubbing Cola on the head and talking directly to her.

Anthony thanked Kendall for listening to his story with such empathy and compassion, and then they watched the movie they had gone to her house to watch. He felt better having shared his story with her. Anthony decided to sleep at his mom's rather than drive all the way back into the city so late. Choosing when to leave Kendall was proving to be quite difficult. That night he had waited until he was too tired to drive back. He knew his mom would not mind having him stay with her for the night. She lived for those kind of surprises.

CHAPTER THIRTEEN

July

K endall could not believe when she woke up that it was already July. It was also a Sunday, so she did not have to head to work, and she was happy about that because *she actually* had a *free day*. Anthony had decided at about 10 o'clock the night before not to head back into the city. After their movie was over Anthony spent the night at his mother's house next door. Tradition still reigned in the neighborhood and especially at the Leone house. However, Kendall had woken up to a text from Anthony and Mama inviting her over for breakfast at nine. She loved big weekend breakfasts because she was usually too rushed getting out of the house on weekdays to grab more than cereal or oatmeal. So, she was heading next door as soon as she put on her day clothes and fixed her hair and brushed her teeth. Mama was so excited to have the "kids" for another day, she went all out for breakfast. She made omelets, sausage patties, bacon, biscuits, and banana and blueberry pancakes. And then she added fresh fruit, yogurt, oatmeal, grits, toast, bagels, cream cheese, jam, maple syrup, honey and whipped butter to the table. And she served it all with orange juice and steaming hot coffee. Kendall was floored with the selection and stuffed when they finished eating.

After breakfast Anthony took Kendall, Mama and Cola to a local park with hiking trails and a beautiful waterfall. The park was located on a lake with picnic tables throughout. They arrived early enough to secure a grill and a picnic table where they could have their picnic. They set up chairs and covered the table with one of Mama's red and white tablecloths. Mama sat in her chair studying the recipes in her notebook and enjoying the sunshine while Kendall and Anthony hiked to the waterfall with Cola. The three of them grilled hotdogs and hamburgers and devoured Mama's famous homemade potato chips and her very own prize dill pickles. Really! Her recipe was the winner at the county fair one year. Anthony confirmed it. Kendall brought watermelon for dessert. It turned out to be "the perfect summer day" and the best way to spend her free time. Kendall loved every moment she spent with them. Anthony still wasn't ready on Sunday evening to head back into the city, but he made himself do it anyway.

After a pleasant and quite relaxing weekend, Kendall headed into work on Monday ready to greet her many customers. July had been a big month for gallery art sales in the past. Summer tourists visiting the city always seemed to love dropping by her gallery as well as many of her customers who made Gallery 116 one of their "must visit" stops on tours with visiting family and friends. Summer visits with new and old customers at the gallery were times she cherished and something she looked forward to each year.

Reign was looking forward to having a somewhat normal, yet busy month ahead. She was starting to understand why Kendall loved summer in the gallery so much. Reign was enjoying the gallery with so many customers coming and going, however she was especially enjoying the slower summer schedule. Kendall seemed less frantic, less stressed and more at peace. They had no special shows or travel scheduled. And she and Branton were getting along well. Reign and Branton had plans to go to the Hamptons to meet his family over the July 4th weekend which she was nervous about, but definitely excited about as well.

Anthony was swamped with work. He had more jobs than he could design for. His customers all needed blueprints before the end of the month to start their building projects before summer's end. Anthony called his mom to complain and to get her perspective on his dilemma. Anthony also wanted to discuss with his mom the email he had received from his condo association that morning.

"Mom, how is it going? I have several things that I wanted to talk over with you. First, I got an email from the condo association for my building this morning. Mom, the building owner wants all of the present tenants in the building to move everything we own into the new condos on the upper floors of the building, so they can renovate the lower ones that are occupied now, like mine. I am furious! I do not have time to pack up everything and move up a few floors. That is ludicrous and should be against building codes and condo policy to require us to comply." Anthony then said just as Billy Joel says in his song, "'Mama, if that is moving up' and if he really can make me do that, 'then I'm moving out.'"

"Anthony, you say you are overwhelmed and stressed with work, and now you have this condo issue. I am a bit worried about you. Why don't you seriously consider moving out here? Kendall and I are both here. You could see us both more often. It is a slower pace out here and you know that. The Presley house is now on the market, you know? You could sell your condo and redo the Presley house using your skills. I know it might be a bit close for us being across the street and all, but I will be sensitive, aware, and I will give you space. I promise! Just think about it!" Mama said smiling as she hung up the phone. "I just might have my boy back in the neighborhood soon if I play my cards right," Mama thought to herself as she finished up the evening dishes.

Anthony called Kendall immediately after the call to his mother. He just needed to hear her voice, and he thought he might discuss a few things with her to get her opinion, as well. Kendall could not believe the plan his condo owner and association had dreamed up. Kendall thought Anthony moving to the neighborhood would be a dream.

"You could even move your practice out here too. You have that option. It is your practice, you know. You will not have the drive in like I do if you do that, and you already have lots of clients out here."

"My mom suggested I look at the Presleys' house. Is that weird? Would that be weird? Is it creepy or too early in our relationship?" Anthony asked awkwardly.

"Of course not! I think it sounds like a dream come true to have you out here every night when I get off work and on weekends. I also think your mom would love it. She's wise, Anthony! You know that! You could save lots of money by moving out of the city too. It could be a fun project remodeling your own house. You have what it takes to take their house down to the studs and to make it into something that reflects you. Reign has her degree in interior design. She and I could both help you with ideas for the inside if you would like or need us to. Let's go see it this week after work. You could drive out with me and ride back in the next morning. "

"I need to have time to think all of this through. You and Mom have given me much to think on."

"Oh, come on, you won't know what you want to do until you see what the house has to offer. Depending on your memory of the inside layout from when you were a kid is nothing to base a big decision on. Deciding to buy the house does not mean you would need to move your practice now. Maybe take things one day at a time and one new idea at a time."

"Ok, I will get the realtor's contact number online and schedule something for Thursday evening just to take a look. Does that work for you?"

"Yes! Absolutely! I'm excited!" said Kendall as she hung up and just as Reign walked into the office.

"Who were you chatting with?" Reign asked curiously.

"Anthony— He is having condo issues, so he is thinking about moving out of the city to my neighborhood, *maybe*. We are looking at a house for him across the street from mine on Thursday if the realtor can schedule a showing."

"Wow! That's a big deal. Things are progressing aren't they, Ken?"

"Yes, yes, they are, and I could not be more thrilled! Sit down and tell me all about your trip to meet Branton's folks. How did that go?" Reign told Kendall every detail of their trip. Things went great with his parents. They loved Reign as Kendall knew they would.

"Branton even discussed getting engaged while we were chatting on the flight home. I could not believe it! I cannot believe it! It all happened so quickly. But don't get me wrong! I would not change a thing! I love him dearly and my parents love him too. I do think he just might really be *the one*," Reign said with joy and hope in her eyes.

On Thursday, Anthony dropped by the gallery at closing time to meet Kendall for the ride out to Hanson Park. He was excited, but he wondered if it would look like he was moving backward by moving back out to the neighborhood where he had grown up. He had worked so hard to build his client base for his architectural firm in the city. Not to mention what it took to secure and purchase his condo in such a prime location years ago. He knew, however, that what other people thought of him was really none of his concern. Those *other people*, whoever they were, did not know the stress *he* had been dealing with, and *they* did not know that the woman he was falling in love with lived *across the street* from where he was looking to move. She was starting to be the only thing, the only person that mattered to him these days, other than his mom, of course.

Anthony agreed with Kendall that the ride out to Hanover Park after work with Kendall was fun. He could get used to that. They listened to Kendall's favorite country music all the way home while she sang her heart out. She played one of her new favorites, "Never 'til now" by Ashley Cooke and Brett Young because it said what she wanted to say but didn't have the guts to say yet. Anthony heard what it said, and it made his heart skip a beat knowing she played it for him.

They were set to meet the realtor at seven, so Kendall ran in to feed Fendy quickly before they walked over to wait on the Presley's porch for the realtor. Mama was going to give them time alone with the realtor and each other, and then she told Anthony she would drop by just to see what he thought about the house.

Anthony and Kendall both loved the house. It had a similar layout to Kendall's. Anthony walked through checking the construction and the foundation. Everything with the structure looked great, but cosmetically the kitchen looked like something he really wanted to update along with all three of the bathrooms. The back porch had a sagging roof that would need to come down. Anthony wanted to enclose the carport and make it a real garage with doors. The yard, especially the back yard needed lots of love, trimming, and clearing out, more than Madge had been able to provide. Overall, it needed work, but he had expected that. He was planning an extensive remodel anyway. No surprises there. It was a dated one-owner home. Anthony needed to sleep on it all, but he was already drawing up plans and hanging his artwork around the house in his mind. Mama arrived just as they were about to leave.

She took a quick walk through the house and said, "What do you think, Son? Do you think it is going to be something you can work with?"

"I really need some time to think it over, Mom, but I do think I can make it work." Mama looked passed Anthony and winked at Kendall.

The next morning before Anthony and Kendall left for work, Anthony had already contacted the realtor asking her to draw up a contract. Anthony's realtor assured him that he would hear from her as soon as she heard back from the Presleys' realtor. If everything went through, the house would be Anthony's by the middle of August. That was a perfect timeline for him because he had to finish up clients' plans first before concentrating on his own blueprints. He would also have to line up a construction company with availability in August which might be quite tricky although he did have great connections, a good reputation for his own work, and some necessary pull for favors owed him.

CHAPTER FOURTEEN

August

K endall's month of August, so far, had been consumed with helping Anthony get his condo ready to sell, helping him pack extra things he wouldn't need while rehabbing the house, and making calls to schedule landscapers, a tree service, and utility companies to get services set up at his new house. Kendall was doing what she could to help.

Anthony hired a construction company that could work with his timeline. The foreman's name was Lance Collier. He was a burly man with red hair and a beard. He was great at his job managing projects. Anthony had worked with him on jobs before, but never on his own, of course. Lance knew when to be serious, but his sense of humor was always begging to be let out. He had played a few tricks on Kendall since the house project began.

One night when Kendall checked in on the crew after work, Kendall walked into Anthony's house to find no one around. She was shocked because she saw the trucks belonging to the crew out front. After several minutes, Lance met her in the kitchen of Anthony's house. Kendall asked where everyone was, and Lance told her that one member of his crew had gotten the chickenpox, so he sent the crew home early.

"Really? Someone on your crew. Someone our age, really?"

"Yes, his name is Grant, He is thirty. He looked terrible, spots everywhere and itching from head to toe."

"Wow! Really? I can't believe that! I hate that for him! When will everyone be back to work? Is it going to slow things down?"

"No, it isn't going to slow anything down. I do not have any guy named *Grant* on my crew. I was just teasing you. You really bought it, didn't you? All the boys are just in the back yard taking a break. We have decided to work late tonight because storms are supposed to come through tomorrow. I was giving them a quick break before starting back up. I think you'd believe anything I say."

On another morning when Kendall stopped in before heading into the gallery. Lance met her at the door and told her that he had just gotten off the phone with a distributor and that all of Anthony's hardwood flooring was on backorder and would not be available until the beginning of November. She was so upset, and she knew Anthony would be far more upset because *that* flooring was the *only* flooring he wanted. He would not be open to choosing something else, and she knew that. Kendall also knew that it would throw off the scheduled move in date and shift the entire deadline considerably. That would mean Anthony would be stuck at Mama's longer than they both expected, which might be a real problem for the two of them, even though they loved each other. Living full time with his mom at 30 was already an adjustment. After watching Kendall process the news on her own for a good ten minutes, Lance admitted that he got her again. The wood flooring just like Anthony had ordered had been delivered, as expected, that morning before Kendall walked over to check in with Lance. Kendall almost kicked him when he revealed the truth. He had gotten her good twice, and Kendall was concerned about how gullible she could be.

She was now on guard when he was around. She was also trying to come up with a plan to get him back. The crew got right to work tearing things down to the studs. They had fun doing that. Anthony and Kendall even got to assist in that chore for a bit one afternoon. Kendall loved the power she felt slinging the big sledgehammer.

Kendall woke up every day, it seemed, even all the way across the street at her house, to the sound of hammers and saws and beeping equipment. If she did not hear that sound, she knew that it was probably a rainy day. She drove home each evening just in time to check the day's progress just before the team left for the day. She thought that it was fun having new activity in the neighborhood. All the neighbors were just as excited as she was to learn of the daily developments. Mama kept everyone up to date and informed since she was closely connected to the project, and she was home every day to watch what happened. She certainly had not been spending as much time writing recipes in her red notebook as of late. She had *other* reasons to keep herself busy now just like everyone else in her life. Anthony had persuaded and finally convinced Mama to dog sit Cola while the condo was on the market. Mama was not accustomed to such rambunctious activity as Cola provided. And she needed to walk *a lot*. Anthony told Mama that exercise was good for her, for Mama that is. He had no one else to take Cola. He was not about to pay for doggie daycare, although he had called Poodley Poodley to see if Jean could help him out at Kendall's request at first, but he had eventually decided that Cola would be better off with Mama. Cola did not need to spend every day at the spa. Anthony was moving out of the city to *save* money. He wasn't about to waste it on spa treatments for his dog, although he did love her and couldn't wait for her to get her own yard. He was having a fence installed as soon as all the big equipment, supplies and materials in the backyard were moved after the house project reached the next phase. Anthony also could not wait to be under the same roof with Cola again. They would be together at Mama's for a while after the condo sold and before he moved into the new house, at least that is what he told Cola and Mama every time he saw them both.

Kendall and Anthony had to make time after work for date nights. They were both busy, but they made time to make each other and their relationship a priority. One special night was spent celebrating Reign and Branton at their engagement party at Pine Valley. The party was given by Reign's parents. And Reign was right, her mom sure could throw a party.

The club was closed for the private event. Reign's mother had worked with Chris to design a Gardener-Fleming signature cocktail for the evening. The bridesmaids and groomsmen sat at their own large table with the future bride and groom. The menu included beef filets, twice-baked potatoes, and asparagus for everyone. The dessert Reign had decided on was heart shaped personal mini chocolate tortes. The flowers on each table were exquisite and coordinating with Reign's chosen color scheme of beige, black and gold. Reign's father's wonderful and meaningful toast kicked off the evening and Kendall's maid-of-honor toast closed out the lovely evening with both laughter and tears.

Kendall and Anthony enjoyed celebrating with everyone but couldn't help wondering when the time might come for them to do the same.

Once Anthony's condo sold, he began living with Mama full time as his house project neared completion. He was finally in the neighborhood daily to answer any questions Lance or any of the crews had for him. Thank goodness because Lance teased Kendall too much, and she fell for it. Lance wouldn't dare try the same with Anthony. He knew better. Anthony wasn't a pretty girl and Anthony was also much too serious about his house project. Anthony being in the neighborhood every day made seeing Kendall more convenient, which he appreciated. She did not feel like it was her responsibility to race home to consult with the crews anymore. Now Anthony was handling that, however she was still rushing home, except now it was just to see Anthony.

Now that the house construction was underway and going well, Anthony felt like he had time to consider moving his firm. It did not seem to be such a daunting decision once the house was progressing. He did not have partners to consider, and all of his office staff already lived in the suburbs. All he really needed to do to get the ball rolling was to find some office space not too far from the new house which he did not think would be too hard to find.

Kendall had assured Anthony that she and Reign would assist him with notifying clients, with changing addresses on all his pertinent office paperwork, with any other ordering of new paperwork, or with any other random office tasks.

Kendall had some extra time and loved helping Anthony, but she also had to stay connected with her artists to encourage their continued creativity. They all seemed to be on good paths creating pieces and delivering them or having them shipped, in Trixie's case. Inglewood was off traveling more like Branton used to do; Susie was painting, but she had just had her first grandbaby; Leslie was in the throes of summer with her kids, so painting for her was occurring but it was sporadic, at best; and Branton was painting so much he was looking for a bigger studio, but he was not in a rush. His mind was a bit muddled with wedding planning now, so the future studio plans just had to wait.

Finally, as the heat of August was at its highest, Anthony's house was under roof and the new air conditioner was cranking out the much-needed cold air for all the hard workers, and there were certainly plenty of workers putting in the work each day. Various teams were in and out from dawn until dusk, installing cabinets, hardwood flooring, new plumbing, and new light fixtures, tiling, painting, building the fence, repairing the back porch, installing the garage doors, and installing all new landscaping. Lance had the teams working together flawlessly. Things seemed to be going along rather quickly and without unnecessary delays. Lance was indeed doing a great job. Anthony had chosen well by going with Lance's company.

Anthony had asked Reign to ride with him out to the house one day to get her thoughts and suggestions on the interior. He had his own ideas, but he wanted to consult with Reign. He knew Reign was qualified and that she was interested in working in the interior design field again one day. He had his regular go-to designers in the city, but he could always use another connection. He knew Reign had style, and he trusted her advice.

While Reign was out of the office and consulting with Anthony, Kendall took that time to pay back Lance for his many practical jokes. Kendall called Lance on his personal cell phone from the gallery phone with a disguised voice claiming to be a county official following up on some permit forms that seemed to be filed incorrectly. Lance sounded flustered and he tried to explain that he thought the woman was mistaken because *all* of *his* forms were approved and hanging at his jobsite on Hanover Lane. In her fake accent Kendall stated, "Sir, I hate to inform you, but you must suspend work on that job immediately. We cannot allow a construction company to proceed without the proper permits. I will consult with my superiors, but until you hear back from me, please do as I say."

Lance reluctantly agreed saying, "Of course, whatever you say," before hanging up and calling Anthony to let him know. Anthony was not happy, to say the least, and he immediately dialed Kendall to let her know. Kendall answered saying, "It isn't true! Anthony, I am sorry you got stuck in the middle on this one, but I had to do it! I had to get Lance back, and I had to get him good! Did it work? Was he angry and concerned?"

"Of course he was! He was furious and totally confused as to what happened with his permits."

"Ok. Now, I feel bad! But I had to do something. He has gotten me too many times. I am sorry I confused and upset you in the process! Will *you* please forgive me? I love you." Kendall said hanging up to dial Lance's number.

"Gotcha!" said Kendall as Lance answered.

"Kendall Fitzpatrick, you are one cruel lady, but you got me good!" Lance said laughing hysterically. "I had no idea that was you, and I was so confused as to what had happened."

Lance placed another call to Anthony explaining Kendall's prank which Lance found funny and then he confirmed that everything would be completed by the end of the month. Anthony thanked him for the update, apologized again for Kendall's prank and then he let Lance get back to work. Despite the prank chaos, Anthony found himself excited about making decisions on things he needed for the interior, so he could be completely moved in by Labor Day. He thought the long weekend was going to be the perfect time to move in, and Mama and Kendall had agreed during earlier discussions about move-in dates. Mama was ready to have her dear boy and his dog out of her hair, and Kendall was ready to have him under his own roof and rules and right across the street for good although she had to admit she was going to miss having Lance in the neighborhood. He had done a great job managing Anthony's project, and he had turned out to be a great guy with a good sense of humor who valued details which Kendall appreciated. That helped Anthony too. They all knew when he completed a job that it was truly complete. He inspected every project his crews completed with a fine-tooth comb and a magnifying glass or so that is how his crews described how he worked. Kendall and Anthony and Mama noticed his attention to detail and appreciated it immensely. It saved Anthony both time and energy.

The condo was sold, so all Anthony had to do was call movers. He had found and rented temporary office space for his architectural firm. Things were happening. He was finally going to be right across the street from Kendall. They were both ready to welcome September and all its changes with open arms. They were hoping that maybe, just maybe, it might bring cooler weather with it when it arrived.

CHAPTER FIFTEEN

September

Anthony and the movers had done all the hard work in the last few days. All Kendall was doing was greeting the moving van with Mama and Cola two days before Labor Day. Their plan was to help Anthony move in and unpack the entire weekend, finishing just in time for a picnic in Larry and Peg's backyard Monday afternoon.

Kendall woke up that morning singing "September Morn" by Neil Diamond. The air in her bedroom felt chilly, even inside for a change. When she opened the back door first thing, there was definitely an early fall chill in the air. She knew it was bound to warm up to hot by the afternoon, but she was starting out the day in jeans and her Yale sweatshirt. It just felt like that kind of morning. She and Mama and Anthony had spent the night cleaning the new construction off of the new house. They removed window stickers and vacuumed up dust and wiped out all the new cabinetry in the kitchen and in each bathroom. Mama had texted to say that she had already deposited Cola in Anthony's newly fenced backyard. Mama was too tired for another day of walking that dog around the neighborhood, especially after their late-night cleaning sesh the night before. Kendall made her coffee, grabbed some oatmeal, and met Mama in Anthony's new front yard. Madge and Larry and Peg and Tish and Harry all ended up there just in time to greet the moving van as it pulled in front of the house right at 10 o'clock. Tish had brought enough warm cinnamon rolls to feed the entire neighborhood and all the movers. Once the doors of the van opened, the activity and excitement didn't stop the entire weekend.

"Son, you've got a whole lotta stuff for one man and a dog. We all better get to unpacking if we are promising to be available to party in two days." Mama said walking toward Anthony's new kitchen with a box cutter and holding her travel mug full of coffee high up in the air. "Good thing I went home to fill *this guy* up again. I'm going to need the energy it gives me to make it to dinnertime. Who's bringing us dinner, anyway? I'm not going to be making a thing. Someone please call Peg and tell her we are desperate. She would love to help us out. That's *her* kind of thing. Do it Kendall, I'm serious! We need all the help we can get even if it means begging for food. We've got to get this boy unpacked in record time, so y'all can go back to work on Tuesday, and so I can drink some spiked lemonade with my friends on Monday."

The moving went off without a hitch. Anthony had clearly marked the contents on each box, and the movers had been extra careful to place each box in the correct room. It just took time to empty all those boxes.

Anthony and Kendall spent lots of time considering where to hang each of Anthony's treasured abstract paintings. He had made sure to design lots of wall space with those pieces in mind. Reign and Branton made the drive out late Saturday and were a great help, especially with hanging artwork.

Peg came through by preparing a taco casserole and salad for the unpacking crew which they consumed throughout the weekend. Mama and Kendall and Anthony worked steadily through the day on Sunday to complete the task in record time by Sunday evening. Anthony was so thankful to be moved in. Mama and Kendall were both glad he was moved in, but they were also glad the work was completed. They were tired. They all had plans to sleep in on Monday only to appear just at party time at the Lawsons. The party was a traditional cookout. Mama was taking potato salad and Anthony and Kendall were providing drinks and chips. It promised to be a low key, casual affair—one that they all needed.

Kendall was back at work bright and early on Tuesday morning after a fun cookout at the Lawson's with all her neighborhood buddies who had quickly become like family. Kendall had gotten to meet Harry's daughter, Cora, who was finally in town for a visit for the holiday. Harry was proud to be able to introduce his daughter to Kendall. Kendall thought Cora was a beautiful girl and pregnancy looked good on her. Cora visited alone, and Kendall was unsure if that was a good or a bad thing. She never got Harry alone long enough to ask.

Anthony had slept three nights in his newly remodeled home, and he and Cola loved it. Anthony was starting Tuesday off looking for properties for his new office location because he was loving being able to stay out of the city every day all day. Not being downtown every day turned out to relieve a lot of his stress.

Anthony's new-found stress-free existence was kind of making Kendall a bit jealous if she was honest. Leaving Anthony every day in the neighborhood to drive into the gallery was wearing on her like never before. She found herself counting down the hours until closing time. She was loving spending her evenings cooking for Anthony and Cola, and even Mama some nights if they weren't eating Mama's delicious traditional Italian fare.

Reign loved helping Anthony choose fabrics and rugs and furniture for his house. She found it fun to use those skills again, but she was happily back at the gallery and planning her wedding for October.

One day at the gallery, a woman walked in with what looked like a very old painting wrapped in a quilt with duct tape. She shared with Kendall and Reign that she had purchased it at a local garage sale but felt like it just might be worth more than she had paid for it which was a mere 10 dollars.

Kendall immediately told the woman that she was not an appraiser, and that they did not have one on staff at the gallery. Kendall said all that before getting a glimpse of the painting. The lady, Mrs. Rashida Taylor, unwrapped the quilt she had around the painting and placed the piece on the front counter. Kendall gasped as soon as she saw the painting. She stepped closer to inspect the brushwork to confirm it was indeed a painting and not a print. It was a simple scene of an older white farmhouse with open windows surrounded by a soft green wide-open stretch of farmland painted in muted tones and neutrals.

"Well, Mrs. Taylor, you do have quite a piece here. Are you looking to sell it, or were you just inquiring about its value?" Kendall asked calmly while taking a labored breath as her heart wildly beat out of her chest.

"I was just curious. It seems nice to me. I'm not sure what I really had in mind. I work down the street and walk past here every day, so I thought today would be the perfect day to bring it in. I am a paralegal, and I do not have much free time. Can you just take the piece, get it appraised, and let me know?"

Kendall said with wide eyes, "We sure can, but I will just need to fill out a quick form and have you sign it before leaving it with us." Kendall walked back to the office, printed off a quick form, filled in the appropriate information and had Mrs. Taylor sign on the dotted line.

"Thank you, girls, so much for helping me out! Just let me know what you find out. All my numbers are on the form." And then Mrs. Taylor walked right out of the gallery.

"Holy Shit, Reign! This is an Andrew Wyeth painting! I cannot believe it! I am certain she could not have even taken the time to google the signature, or she would have known," said Kendall loudly. And then Kendall paused and said out loud, "I am just so stunned and confused!"

"I'm not an art historian, and I have even heard of Wyeth. *Christina's World* is iconic. Holy crap! What do we do now?"

Kendall said, "We start taking pictures of every angle front and back. I am going to the office to contact Sotheby's and Christie's straight away."

Kendall came back out of the office several minutes later as Reign said, "And? What did you find out?"

"I found out that we need to lock our doors tonight and make certain that the alarm is set. No, really, I found out that they need the photos. They will look at them and most likely send out a specialist in the next few days to discuss estimates. I want to hire a local appraiser first before Sotheby's or Christie's sends their people. I want to have a ballpark estimate and a confirmation by an expert, so I do not go into this blindly."

"Good idea," said Reign excitedly. "This has started September out right. Don't you think?"

Kendall was still floored. People had brought in pieces asking about them before, but something like this had never happened at Gallery 116. "Call Branton! I do not want to make a big deal about it because it is not ours, but Branton will *want* to see *this*."

Branton showed up within the hour, and he too was stunned. He just stared at the piece pouring over every inch for at least a good half hour.

Anthony called later in the afternoon to tell of his office space search, so she spilled the beans about *their* excitement for the day too. He was excited for her. It was a big deal for a gallery owner with an art history background. Anthony shared that he potentially found the perfect permanent office space for sale about ten minutes from the neighborhood. He wanted to schedule time with her to take her through the space. It was being vacated by the current owners at the end of September.

Kendall drove out of the city that night without dreading the drive for the first time in weeks. The day had been surprising and exciting. And it breathed some life into her. She was thankful to have the down time to listen to music on the way home to see Anthony even though a nasty tropical storm was passing through with torrential downpours. She couldn't wait to cozy up on her couch with Fendy, Cola and Anthony after dinner. She had put a roast in her crockpot before leaving for work, so a yummy dinner would be ready and waiting for her when she got home. She was learning that it pays off to plan dinners, so she isn't ever stuck eating cereal for dinner ever again unless cereal was what she wanted to have for dinner of course.

Kendall could not wait to get into the gallery the next day just to see that painting with her very own eyes one more time. After unlocking the door, Kendall ran to the office where she was glad to see it still hidden under her desk wrapped in bubble wrap and brown paper with cardboard on the outside for protection where she had stashed it. She hated to mess up the packaging, but she opened it just to get a glimpse before Reign arrived. Kendall was certain to receive a call from both auction houses sometime during the day, and her appraiser would be at the gallery at two. Kendall turned on the radio for some company while she was alone in the gallery. The deejays kept interrupting with reports of the storm that had been passing through the area and causing lots of flash flooding. It was a big one, a wide tropical system, and it was causing destruction as it roared up the East Coast.

When the appraiser arrived just before 2, Kendall greeted him at the door and showed him to the counter where the painting was awaiting authentication. "You say this piece was purchased at a yard sale. Do you know where that was? If so, I'm assuming we have no idea of the painting's provenance. Because of that I will need to do more extensive research at my office after I leave today. For now, I will examine the piece, the brushstrokes and the signature. I would also like to remove it from the frame to see what might be written on the back and to see what this one was actually painted on. Artists used to use a variety of surfaces other than canvases, and also various types of paint. I will be able to tell quite a bit upon examination. Andrew Wyeth was known to use egg tempera on panels. We will see what we have here shortly," he said as he began the process of removing the frame.

Kendall and Reign watched the appraiser's every move. Good thing they did not have any other customers during his appointment time. He left over two hours later having confirmed that it was indeed a Wyeth. As for the actual valuation, that would have to come later after his further research. He promised to get back to Kendall by the next morning. She still had not received confirmation from the auction houses as to when they were sending representatives. The women she spoke to at both auction houses mentioned that they may just accept the paperwork from her appraisal to start the process of offering the painting for auction if Mrs. Taylor chooses to go that route. Kendall and Reign had not gotten the impression from her that she was a real art connoisseur, so they were pretty confident she would be willing to sell, and Kendall was hoping that either Sotheby's or Christie's would send a qualified representative to inspect the piece before shipping.

At 4:07, Cait's parents, Frank and Gloria Connor came bursting into the gallery. Kendall looked up from the front counter shocked and surprised to see them in the gallery. They had not visited there since it's opening night years ago. "What brings you two by?" Kendall asked while spotting tears in Gloria's eyes.

"Well, Kendall, we came to share some really bad news with you. Cait and Toby were out on a date night last night. They left Harper with a babysitter, thank goodness!" Gloria said, beginning to get choked up.

Frank continued. "Their car was overtaken by flood waters in downtown Philly as Tropical Storm Uri passed through late last night. Their car was found, but Cait and Toby did not survive. The police called us this morning to let us know. Harper is still with the babysitter. We are on our way to get her there now."

Kendall started to sob thinking of all the good times she and Cait had shared, and she thought about their last conversation in person in March just before Cait had moved. They had chatted about the transition and their new house a few times on the phone since the move, but Kendall had not seen her in person since March. Kendall suddenly felt numb. And then she thought about Harper, precious Harper no longer having parents. Kendall hugged Frank and then Gloria. Gloria did not want to let go. Kendall knew they were devastated. Cait was their only child. And Kendall was the closest thing to Cait now at that moment and she would be, until they had Harper in their arms.

"Is there anything I can do for you?" Kendall asked as Reign walked in on the scene.

"We would really love it if you could go with us to Philadelphia. We are not sure what all is going to be involved with our trip, and we will be responsible for Harper the entire time, from now on really. Come with us! We could really use your help," Gloria said wiping her eyes.

Reign had heard enough to guess the situation. "Ken, if you need to go anywhere. You know I can handle things here."

Frank said, "We are heading to the airport shortly, so we don't have much time."

"I have my Pilates bag packed with all my essentials— a new toothbrush and several changes of clothes. You can take that with you. Really! Just go! I will let everyone know where you had to go. Do it for Harper!" Reign declared.

"We can buy your ticket on the way to the airport. The flight wasn't full when we made our reservations a few hours ago. Come, go with us! We would so appreciate the company," said Gloria.

Kendall agreed, headed to the restroom and then grabbed Reign's bag, her own purse and her phone. She did not have a clue what the next few days might hold, but after losing her mother, she had a clue. She did not know if she was ready. She was still devastated and in shock. She took one big breath before she hugged Reign and headed out the door with Gloria and Frank. She booked her plane ticket in the car and texted Anthony about the news and her sudden plans to fly to Philly. She made sure he knew to check in on Fendy and to feed her twice a day. Kendall was so thankful for Anthony, especially on days like this one.

Arriving at Cait's home to pick up Harper from the babysitter was harder than any of them could have imagined. It was late, so they packed a few things for Harper, let the babysitter go home, and then headed to the hotel where Kendall finally got to call Reign and Anthony to tell them how hard things really were. She could be honest with them both. They hated Kendall had to go through this, especially so soon after losing her own mom. Harper was in the room with her grandparents, so after her phone calls, Kendall stretched out on the bed, put in her headphones and listened to the song, "You Can't Make Old Friends" as she tried to relax and unwind from the crazy day. Kendall felt and processed her feelings by listening to music. Good lyrics had a way of healing her soul, like all other types of art. That night was no different. That song made her cry, cry so hard, she fell asleep on a tear-soaked pillow.

Their time in Philadelphia was busy and successful. They were able to find Toby and Cait's will, designating Cait's parents as the legal guardians if anything were to happen to Cait and Toby. Frank and Gloria were not surprised to read it, but to say they were ready for all it entailed was another story. Frank and Gloria had one brief court hearing to make everything official, they had movers pack up everything that belonged to Toby and Cait, and they put the house on the market, and took Harper to see her pediatrician to get her records before taking her back to the Conners to live full time. It was a whole lot to accomplish in three days' time, but miracles do happen, and they had.

Kendall was weary and worn out, but she was back at work by the end of the week. She was working first thing on the Wyeth painting. Her local appraiser had gotten back to her on the painting's valuation, so she would be well informed when the representative from Christie's showed up that afternoon. He valued the painting at anywhere from three to four million. Now whether Christie's thought they could get that for it at auction was yet to be determined. Kendall was astounded, but she wasn't about to contact Mrs. Taylor until she knew everything she needed to know after her afternoon appointment.

Kendall had really missed Anthony while she was gone. In fact, she had spent the night with him the night before when she got back in town. She had never done that before, but she was sad, still sad and had not wanted to spend another night alone. The nights in the hotel were hard enough. She was finding nights alone harder and harder to handle since meeting Anthony. Kendall had not gotten to tour the office location with Anthony because of her trip, but he was all set to move in at the beginning of October after the closing and after the present owners moved out. His employees were really excited about the move. It would not be a big change for Anthony because he had been working out of both his house and the temporary office space for several weeks now. His clients had not minded at all and neither had he although everyone was looking forward to the official opening of his new permanent office location.

Anthony attended Cait and Toby's memorial service with Kendall for extra support and comfort. It was a hard thing for him to do. It brought back bad memories, but he was glad to do it *for Kendall*. Kendall survived it with Anthony by her side. Seeing a few old friends there that she had not seen in many, many years made it easier to handle. Seeing Cait's and Toby's parents in such pain tore at Kendall's heart. Kendall felt for Harper too. Harper had stayed home with another babysitter because she was far too young to attend. Kendall did wish she could have given Harper one last big hug though. That little girl's life had just been turned upside down, and it broke Kendall's heart again thinking about it.

After the service, Kendall had to go straight back to work. She needed to focus. She had been having so many important distractions, but it was time she got to work because Reign was taking several weeks at the end of September and into October off from the gallery for in-depth wedding planning and house searching with Branton and Kendall wanted to be all caught up with her work when she did. Reign and Branton's wedding was set for October the 14th. The two of them were planning to move out to the suburbs too after the wedding, but they were looking at newer neighborhoods with larger lot sizes. Branton was still interested in a larger studio space, so they were looking at both houses with room to add on and houses with property with space to build a possible free-standing studio. Kendall and Anthony were super excited to have them close by. Both couples enjoyed spending time with each other.

On September 21st, Kendall was in the gallery alone. It had been a slow day when Frank and Gloria walked in without Harper. Kendall was scared to death. She wondered where Harper was and more importantly, she wondered why they were at the gallery again. It brought back bad memories seeing them walk in, but she tried to seem unfazed.

"Hey, guys! How are you both?" How can I help you? Kendall asked curiously.

"Well, Ken, the reason for our being here might shock you, again. We did not want to call you on the phone, but we have something very important to discuss with you." Frank said very seriously.

"Kendall, as you know, Frank and I are not spring chickens. This "taking care of a baby" thing has been hard on us, especially after losing Cait. We love Harper with everything we have as any grandparents would. We are just concerned about being older. I mean things have really, really changed since we had Cait, and we are very concerned that we will not be giving her the best life if she grows up with us. We think she needs younger parents like her parents were. Do you understand?"

"Yes, I think I do," Kendall said cautiously not knowing what was coming next.

"That is why we are here to see you today. We know you are not married, but that you have a very serious boyfriend. We are aware of all of that. And we have taken that into consideration. Would you consider taking over custody of Harper? We would still be full-time grandparents and help in whatever way we can. We would pay for any of the legal fees incurred for you to obtain full custody," said Frank.

Gloria added, "We know that you probably cannot give us an answer today. We are willing to give you the time you need to make the best decision for you and for Harper. We have prayed all about this, and we feel like we are making the best decision for our granddaughter. I hope we have not completely upset you for the rest of your day. Please know we would not spring this on you if we did not think it was in Harper's best interest."

"Oh no! Do not worry about me. This is not really about me, anyway. I will need some time to take this all in however, and time to talk this over with several people in my life who will be affected by my decision. I hope you all can understand that. I will let you know as soon as I can. I promise! And I appreciate you thinking enough of me to ask."

"Ken, you were Cait's best and oldest friend. You already are Harper's godmother. Toby and Cait chose you for that role for a reason. I know they would approve, and we know in our hearts that you are the perfect person for the job, and the job it will be. Raising kids isn't a walk in the park, even though parents do spend a lot of time in parks," said Frank trying to make light of a very serious conversation. They all hugged, and Kendall promised to get in touch and then, just like that, she was alone in the gallery again.

"How did I get here? I was just asked to become a mother instantly and just a few weeks after losing my best childhood friend in the same year of losing my own mom," Kendall thought to herself as she slid down the side of the counter to the floor where she curled up into a ball to cry her eyes out, once again. If she did agree to all of this, it was going to require more time, more maturity, and more resources than she thought she had. She was going to have to make more room in her life than she had first thought at the beginning of this wild rollercoaster of a year. "And to think adopting Fendy a few years back had been a big deal for me at the time. Wow, times have really changed and changed me in the process," said Kendall out loud to herself alone in the gallery.

After Kendall spent a bit of time on the floor, she realized that she was in fact in the gallery, and that she needed to act like a mature adult and like a professional on the job and to get herself off of the gallery floor.

She got off the floor and went to freshen up before her afternoon appointment with the representative from Christie's. It was on a day like today when Kendall wished she could just call up her mom. She also wished Reign was at work and not taking time off. "I could use a friend in the gallery today," Kendall thought to herself.

As it turned out, Gina, the rep for Christie's was indeed qualified and a true expert in her field. Gina was impressed with the painting and confirmed that it was indeed a Wyeth like she had been told and as Kendall had determined on her own. She asked Kendall to ship the painting to the New York office after having it insured for the shipping process. Gina suggested a reliable and professional shipper that offered crating whom Kendall had used many times before. Gina assured her that after things were confirmed in the main office, Christie's could provide auction paperwork and a contract, and they would be able to confirm an auction starting price which she assumed would be around $300,000, but the selling price would probably be somewhere between four and five million dollars. At least, that is what Gina was estimating according to previous sales of Wyeth's pieces of similar size.

As soon as Gina left, Kendall walked back to the office to make a call to Mrs. Taylor and to Anthony, sure to be two very important and shocking calls. Mrs. Taylor had zero idea what she had actually purchased for ten dollars, and Anthony would not be expecting Kendall to share the news about the Connors' visit to the gallery. What a day it had turned out to be.! Oh, and she had to call Reign and inform her of all the new developments. She had promised not to bother her, but these were exceptions. Maybe Reign would have some updates of her own.

Mrs. Taylor screamed and dropped the phone after Kendall caught her up to speed on what she had found out about Mrs. Taylor's painting. After picking up the phone once again, Mrs. Taylor said, "Lord, have mercy, Girl! Are you really telling me I'm about to get very wealthy?"

"Yes, ma'am I am! It does look that way. I will get the final figures from Christie's next week. Then, you will need to decide if you want to proceed to sell it at auction. It will ensure you get the highest price. They will notify art collector's all over the world alerting them that it will be coming up for auction."

"Proceed? You better bet I do! This has turned out to be the best ten dollars I have ever spent. And I am all for turning it into more money in record time. Proceed, Kendall! Let me know what I need to do next."

"I will probably need you to drop by in the next few days to fill out and sign an auction contract," Kendall said thanking her for coming to the gallery for help. "Reign and I have had such fun with the process! Thanks for including us!"

"Oh, you bet! I will make it worth your effort when all is said and done. I assure you!" And the two ladies hung up their call.

Kendall took a big deep breath and dialed Anthony's number.

Anthony answered saying, "Hey, Babe, how is everything going?"

"Well, today has certainly been interesting. The Connors came into the gallery again today."

"Really? Did you get to see Harper?" Anthony asked curiously not knowing where the conversation was headed.

"No, I didn't. She was not with them. They came for a serious chat and left her with a friend. Anthony, you will not believe what they asked me. I wanted to tell you in person tonight, but I just can't wait. They want me to take over custody of Harper. They feel that they are a bit too old to start parenting again. They know that it is now ultimately their responsibility, but after a few weeks they realize that they are not up for it like they previously thought. They feel like I'm the perfect person to take the job over. I am a bit embarrassed to even be telling you this. I'm sure you think it is a wild idea. It could ruin our relationship if we add a child in the mix at this point and all."

"Actually, Ken, I think it is a wonderful opportunity for you, for us. We are serious, I think. I mean, we have certainly talked about marriage in the future. This way, when we do get married, we will be one child ahead. That could be perfect. You are her godmother. Toby and Cait chose *you* for a reason. I know you work now, but Mama and the other ladies in the neighborhood would all help out. Tish is even a pediatric nurse. I mean all the ladies raised great kids. I'm one of those. Ha-ha! I'm not trying to persuade you to do it, it must be your decision first and foremost, but I'm just sayin', it wouldn't be the worst thing. She *is* a super cute little girl. She *is* just nine months old. *And* she *did* just lose *both* of her parents."

"Wow! I never could have imagined this being your reaction. I still must think about it a bit. I want to run it by my dad and Reign first to get their opinions of me with a nine-month-old baby. They know me well too, and they will both be honest."

Kendall called her father next. He was more excited than she would have ever imagined too. He always loved Cait; he loved their friendship; and because he loved Kendall, he thought taking over custody would be a beautiful thing to do with her life. He also mentioned that he thought her mother would have agreed.

Kendall then checked in with Reign.

"Hey, Girl!" Reign said answering the phone. I have been meaning to call you all day. Branton and I found a house! It doesn't have a studio or room for one, but the house is beautiful. We love it! It is only about five minutes from your neighborhood. We will move in just after the wedding. I cannot take on a move before the wedding. Why are *you* calling? I know it *must* be important.

"For two reasons—Christie's got back to me. The estimated price for the painting to sell at auction is between four and six million. And, the Connors asked me to assume custody of Harper."

"Holy crap, Ken! No wonder you called! Those are huge reasons to call. Is Mrs. Taylor letting the painting go to auction? And how do you feel about taking Harper in now and eventually adopting her one day? That is one hefty commitment. Have you talked it over with Anthony? I'm sure he has an opinion."

"Mrs. Taylor is going to auction with the piece and believe it or not, Anthony was not against the idea. I was floored. I still have lots of thinking and overthinking to do before I can possibly make a decision. So much has happened this year and now this."

"Yea, but consider Harper without a mom, a real mom like you, for the rest of her life if you don't step in. You have experienced only a few months without yours. And you are very much like her mom. Y'all were best friends and the exact same age. Just think what you could offer her. It would be a very selfless act, and you would reap unimaginable rewards."

Kendall got off the phone and just sat at her desk going over in her head what everyone had shared with her. She sat in silence for a while, then she got up, locked the gallery doors and headed home for the evening. She listened to "Sweetest Devotion" by Adele and "Isn't She Lovely" by Stevie Wonder on the way home to chat with Anthony face to face and to make her decision. She would need to make a decision sooner rather than later, for the Conners and Harper and for Anthony who needed her help to get ready to move into his new office space soon. She wanted to be focused for him, and not have her mind in a million different places trying to make big life changing decisions.

Chapter Sixteen

October

N ow that it was October, real fall was in the air. Leaves were changing and so was Kendall's life. Kendall had helped Anthony, his mom and his employees move in and get settled at his new office just minutes from the neighborhood. Anthony was thrilled with how the office set up turned out. The style and design of the building, although he did not design it, represented his design style. The inside of the office was sleek, chic and sophisticated. He was proud. And so was Mama to have him so close every day if she needed him for anything, even for a quick visit so she could see his face.

Kendall was in full swing as Reign's maid of honor. She had ordered and received her gold dress, attended a local bachelorette weekend, and had thrown and attended several bridal showers for Reign. The wedding was two weeks away. Reign was as frazzled as expected, and Kendall was doing all she could to help,

After two weeks of thinking things through, Kendall had finally contacted the Connors letting them know that they could start drawing up the paperwork to transfer custody of Harper to Kendall. Mr. Gardener, Reign's father, was assisting Kendall with her part of the paperwork and he would be the one to handle the official adoption paperwork and hearing which would not go through until November or December. Kendall had completed her home study and was expected to get temporary custody on the 6th of October, so her evenings were being spent with Anthony converting her "making room" guest room into a nursery for Harper.

One night in bed snuggling with Fendy, Kendall whispered to Fendy about her getting a big sister. Fendy purred immediately, and Kendall took that as a sign of approval. Kendall had been worrying about how Fendy and even Cola would adapt to having a small human around.

Before the Connors brought Harper over to officially live with Kendall, Anthony thought it would be a good time to take Kendall away for a weekend to celebrate their fall birthdays. Anthony had rented a cabin in the mountains with a large fireplace. He paid for an extra service to stock the fridge and prepare several meals upon their arrival, so it could be a real break for them both. Things were about to change in their lives, and they wanted to be ready and relaxed when it did. The nursery was completed, and work was going well for the both of them. Anthony's new office was a fun place to work, but getting away to have Kendall all to himself was priceless. This was a weekend to celebrate their relationship, before Kendall became a mom. They spent the weekend going to a fall festival and an arts and crafts show, drinking fresh hot apple cider, eating cider donuts with every meal, reading books by their favorite authors and sleeping in and going to bed early. On the drive home they even stopped at a pumpkin patch to purchase mums and pumpkins to decorate both of their front porches and for his office and for her gallery.

The 6th arrived before she knew it, and of course Kendall had decided to stay home from work to get Harper all settled in. She had the whole day, since it was Friday, and the weekend too to spend with her. Anthony was closing his office early too, just to spend time with the two of them. Mama and her friends were providing a meal to be delivered in the evening when the neighbors planned to come by to meet Harper in person.

The Connors arrived at Kendall's house around 10 o'clock in the morning with Harper and all her belongings and baby must-haves. Harper was dressed in a pink, long sleeve jumper with a little pink hat on her head to match. Gloria's tears were rolling down her cheeks as she handed a giggling and smiling Harper over to Kendall. Harper was happy and Gloria was sad, but Gloria knew she and Frank were doing what they had to do. They all knew that this decision was for the best for everyone involved, especially Harper.

"Would you like for us to carry these things back to her new room?" Gloria asked. Gloria handed Kendall a picture of Cait and Toby she thought Kendall might want to have for Harper one day.

"Thank you for the photo. I will put it in a safe place for her. Sure, I would love for you both to see her new room," said Kendall. "Come on back!" Kendall had painted the room pink and had chosen a butterfly theme for all the tiny details. She even ordered a special mobile with various colored butterflies that she already had hanging over the crib. "Branton and Susie, two of my artists, painted the paintings hanging on the walls in here. They are very special to me because *they* painted them and because they match so perfectly."

"It is adorable! She is going to love *playing* and *sleeping* in here. It is just perfect! Cait would have loved this for her. You know Cait loved butterflies."

"Yes ma'am, that is *why* I decided on this theme! I thought it was the perfect way to keep her memory alive."

Leaving Harper's room, Gloria asked if Kendall needed Frank to help her install Harper's car seat. Gloria said he had been officially trained on how to properly install one by a police officer friend. Kendall agreed that it would help quite a bit since she wasn't sure how to install one correctly. Gloria placed a copy of Harper's medical records on Kendall's front hall table as they all walked out to Kendall's car in the carport.

After Frank installed the car seat, the Connors hugged and kissed Harper, hugged and thanked Kendall promising to keep in touch often, especially since her custody was not final. Kendall just had temporary custody until the next hearing.

Anthony seemed to be turning into Kendall with his music to soothe his soul. He listened to "Daughters" by John Mayer on his short drive home that day. Anthony arrived at Kendall's house a little after one. He was so excited to be greeted at Kendall's door by Kendall and Harper. He was surprised by just how cute and friendly she was. She reached out to be held in his arms immediately. Kendall knew in that moment that somehow Harper was already wrapped around his finger. The three of them spent the rest of the afternoon playing and bonding with each other. They even took Harper for a long walk in the neighborhood. Kendall and Anthony were both shocked at how easily she went down for a nap afterwards. Her nap gave the two of them time to chat about his day and to pick up the house in time for the dinner delivery crew that was set to arrive sometime after Harper's nap.

At five o'clock on the dot Harper woke up just as Mama and her neighbor buddies knocked on the door carrying and delivering loads of food, their dinner—lots of it—enough for an army.

"We know we have a lot here, but you can freeze any leftovers," said Mama followed by Madge, Tish, Peg, Larry and Harry carrying gift bags for Harper and Kendall. They were all there to meet Harper. They knew the joys of bringing a baby home, and they had not forgotten the feeling. They wanted to celebrate. They were thrilled for Kendall and Anthony and Harper too knowing Kendall would be a loving and caring and supportive mother.

Tish spoke for the group saying, "We all want you to know how happy we are for you, Ken. We wanted to come here tonight to welcome Baby Harper into the neighborhood and into all our lives. We brought you dinner and a few baby gifts. We won't stay long. Just know that we are all here for you, for whatever you might need. I know I am certainly available for around the clock baby health questions if you ever have those."

Mama chimed in saying, "And it really goes without saying, but I'm always available to babysit, during work or for date nights, whatever is needed."

The group quickly filed out after Kendall opened the gifts just as quickly as they filed in. Each person admired Harper again as they walked out. Harper was going to have a happy life if these neighbors had anything to do with it. They had lots of love to give and lots of time to show and to share that love.

Kendall felt comfortable the first several days taking care of Harper. Harper was a great eater and a great sleeper. Anthony had made everything easier by hanging out at Kendall's house every waking hour for support just in case she needed it. Mama kept Harper at Kendall's on Monday just so Kendall could get back to work since it was the week of Reign and Branton's wedding and Kendall had no one else to open the gallery.

Friday night arrived quickly. It was Reign and Branton's rehearsal and rehearsal dinner. Anthony and Kendall both attended, and they took Harper with them to the rehearsal and to the dinner that followed. Anthony gladly held Harper during the practicing part of the evening and Harper slept in her car seat during the entire dinner which shocked and amazed Anthony, Kendall and everyone else in attendance. Reign had been far too busy lately to visit and to meet Harper, but as soon as Reign laid eyes on Harper at the rehearsal, she adored her.

For the wedding the next evening, Mama, Peg and Tish planned a girls' night at Kendall's so they could spend time with Harper. Anthony was all dressed up in his suit when he left all three of the ladies chatting and taking turns cuddling Harper. Anthony was meeting Kendall at St. Paul's Episcopal where the wedding was taking place. Kendall had reported to the church at nine that morning for her maid of honor duties of being by Reign's side all day for pictures and for support. Anthony was stunned when Kendall greeted him in the back of the church dressed in her gold dress with her hair down and curled loosely. He, once again, thought she was the most stunning woman he knew. He was very proud to be by her side and receive a special "hello kiss" before the ceremony started.

The wedding turned out just as beautiful as Reign and her parents and Branton had planned. The church was decorated to perfection and the reception held at the country club afterwards was top-notch thanks to Josh and Stephanie, the club's special event team. Kendall and Anthony had tons of fun celebrating with the happy couple, but not as much fun as going home to relieve the three sitters of their duties once the wedding was over. Kendall and Anthony changed out of their fancy clothes and into sweats, put Harper in her pajamas and then the three of them cozied up by the fire with one sippy cup of warm milk and two hot cups of cocoa.

Kendall's father, Arthur, was expected the next morning for a quick visit to meet Harper. He had a planned visit for Christmas, but he could not wait until then to meet his new granddaughter. Kendall and Anthony and Harper were picking him up at the airport. Kendall had been worried about where her father would sleep, since Harper's nursery was where her guest room used to be, but Mama and Anthony assured her that her father could stay in one of their many extra bedrooms.

Kendall loved introducing her father to Anthony and Harper. They sat around all afternoon after getting home from the airport chatting, getting acquainted, and playing with Harper. Arthur was proud of Kendall, and he certainly approved of Anthony. Arthur thought he seemed to be a much better fit for Kendall than Colin ever was. He just wished his wife could have joined them all. He knew Joan would also have been proud of Kendall for her latest life choices.

Mama had plans to cook dinner for everyone after Arthur had spent the day with Kendall and Harper. It didn't take long for Kendall's dad to adore Harper, and she appeared to adore him quickly too. Her father had brought a few of Kendall's baby dresses and a few of her favorite childhood toys with him for Kendall to have at her house now that she had a daughter of her own. One of the dresses was for Harper's current size, so Kendall dressed her in that dress along with matching tights and the four of them walked over to Mama's house around five. Arthur was tickled pink to see Harper wearing one of Kendall's dresses. He remembered the day Kendall had worn it like it were yesterday and he enjoyed getting to see Harper wear it too.

Kendall could not wait to introduce her father to Mama. She knew they were two special people that just might appreciate each other.

The smells of onions, garlic, tomato sauce and warm bread overwhelmed their senses as they walked in the back door of Mama's house. Kendall and Anthony introduced their parents, the ones they still had around, and then helped Mama get the food on the table.

Everyone had fun chatting over dinner. The food was enjoyed by everyone, as expected. Harper loved the highchair of Anthony's that Mama dug out of storage. Surprisingly it was in good condition. Harper seemed to like sitting at the table amongst all of the excitement and conversations eating bananas and pieces of fresh warm bread. After dinner, Mama convinced Arthur to sleep in one of her guest rooms since she was just next door to Kendall and Harper. To Kendall's surprise, he had agreed. Anthony was shocked Mama had offered, with her father being a man and all. But Anthony had noticed that her mom did seem to enjoy Kendall's father's company.

The next morning Anthony arrived at Kendall's around 9:30 to see her and Harper and expected to see Arthur with the girls, but he was nowhere in sight.

"Where is your dad? I figured he would be over here by now."

"Me too! I was going to go over to your mom's house to check on him when you got here. I assumed he would have been back over here by now. It is late for him. He is a big morning person."

"I will run next door and check on them. Do you mind if Cola stays here with you both? If not, she can run with me."

"Cola can stay. I will formally introduce her to Harper while you are gone. Hopefully, she will like Harper more than Fendy does currently. Since Harper arrived Fendy spends her days hiding underneath my bed. She is trying to make a point I think."

Anthony walked next door and into his mom's house only to hear roaring laughter coming from the kitchen. "What are you two doing in here? Sounds like fun," said Anthony as he walked into the kitchen.

Mama quickly said, "I made Arthur breakfast, and now we are just chatting and having more coffee. We were just about to play gin rummy. How are the girls this morning?"

"They are good. I came over because Kendall was just worried about where Arthur was since she had not seen him all morning," said Anthony looking over at Arthur.

"Oh, please tell her I am sorry. We have been having such fun chatting and getting to know each other. Your mother is not short on words as I'm sure you know, and I have really missed having company in the mornings, so I'm enjoying our time together." Arthur confessed sadly. "If you think I need to rush over, I will. I don't want it to look like I have abandoned my daughter."

"No worries. You both enjoy your morning. I will tell Kendall that you both are fine and that you are enjoying yourselves and that you, Arthur, will see her a bit later," Anthony said heading back out the door.

Reign and Branton arrived back in town from their honeymoon to Hawaii just after Kendall's father left to head back to Phoenix. Kendall had loved her father's visit, and she thought he had enjoyed his time too meeting Harper, Anthony and Mama. He said that he could not wait to come back at Christmas time, and they could not wait to have him back. It seemed as though he would be staying at Mama's again on his next visit. They had a lot in common, even cooking show watching. They apparently offered each other much needed companionship, and Anthony and Kendall weren't sad about it.

Anthony and Kendall spent the next weekend helping Reign and Branton move into their new home just as they had helped with Anthony's move. Their new home was close by, a much bigger new colonial painted white with a black door. It had a large, fenced backyard with a swimming pool and the kitchen was state-of-the-art. There were plenty of bedrooms for a nursery and future nurseries. Branton had been wanting a dog for a while. Kendall thought that with a fenced yard, he might just have an easier time convincing Reign now. Since Reign and Branton were combining households, they had way more stuff than Anthony had in his move. Their hired movers were being paid to move and to unpack as well, so it lightened the load. Because of that they had many more hands than expected, and the task was completed by Saturday night.

After helping with the move, Kendall woke up on Monday morning tired, sore and actually a bit nervous about heading to her custody hearing that day where Kendall was expected to be awarded full custody of Harper. Anthony was going with her for support, and she would be meeting Mr. Gardener and the Conners at the courthouse. It was a big day, but a day she was so glad had arrived. The decision to take over custody of Harper had been one of the best decisions of her life. Kendall and Anthony had been able to make room for her and Harper fit just right, like the perfect puzzle piece.

Kendall had indeed been granted full custody, and she was ecstatic. The Conners were thankful and again promised to keep in touch. Anthony took Harper home to stay the rest of the day with Mama on his way back to work, so Kendall could go into the gallery for a bit. Susie was the one who had been watching the gallery as needed lately with Reign away. Reign was due back the next day, however. Susie was an *attendant only* at the gallery, and Kendall did not expect her to work in the office, make sales or oversee other business. That is why Kendall was spending the afternoon working—to get *actual* work done. Kendall had mail to open, bills to pay, and customer calls to return. Kendall still cared for the gallery, so she had to make some sacrifices to make sure it continued to be a success. She was having a very difficult time handling much from home since she had no office there now. She also needed to show art to sell art and that wasn't possible unless she was at the gallery around the actual paintings to discuss them with customers.

Reign was still interested in working at the gallery, but she wanted to get back into interior design one day. Kendall had been thinking about how she could help. Kendall had decided to give all the designers over to Reign so that she could collaborate exclusively with them handling all their client needs. That would keep Reign up to date on the latest design trends, and it would provide her with connections that she might find valuable down the road.

The gallery phone began ringing as Kendall finished up her other tasks. "Hello, Gallery 116, may I help you?"

"This is Gina Coulter, the representative for Christie's. I am just following up after the auction. Did you hear the news? Did you happen to watch the auction on our website?"

"No," said Kendall. "Things have been very busy here. Did the painting sell?

"Yes, it did, for way more than what we expected! Your client's painting sold for 6.7 million dollars! Can you believe it? I am calling to see if you want to contact Mrs. Taylor or if you would like for me to do that?"

"Actually, I believe that it may mean more to Mrs. Taylor if you call to inform her. Be prepared because she will scream on the phone. I have no doubt," Kendall said laughing. Kendall felt Rashida would more likely believe Gina, and then Rashida and Gina could discuss where to send the check or where to automatically deposit the sale amount because Kendall really had nothing to do with the auction part or the sale at all. She had only connected Rashida with Christie's and Gina. Kendall was only the middleman in this case, sadly. Kendall thought that maybe she should frequent garage sales more often as she got off the phone, knowing full well that what had happened with that ten-dollar painting was a rare and wild once in a lifetime find that would change Mrs. Taylor's life forever.

It had been good hearing back from Gina, but Kendall needed to quickly close the gallery and head home. It was her first Halloween with Harper, and it was Anthony's first Halloween since he moved back to the neighborhood. Kendall rushed home to get dressed in her costume and to get Harper dressed too. Anthony begged Kendall to dress Harper as Pebbles. Kendall agreed. She would be Wilma and Harper would be Pebbles. Anthony was reviving his high school Fred Flintstone costume to complete the family look. After everyone was dressed, Mama arrived to take photos before they started their rounds in the neighborhood. Mama's plan was to stay at her house as she always had. Her tradition was to hook up a speaker on her porch to play "Monster

Mash" while she dressed in her chef's hat and passed out home-made popcorn balls to all the costumed visitors.

Hanover Park had always been known as the traditional Hal-loween neighborhood. It was picture perfect like the scene from a classic fall movie. This night was no different. The porch lights were lit on every house, there was a chilly fog in the air and there were children with their families walking up and down the streets dressed in costume and carrying jack-o-lantern buckets filled with candy. Anthony, Kendall and Harper stopped over at Mama's house first off. They could hear Mama chatting with all the children from the sidewalk as they walked toward her door. Anthony could not wait to get his hands on one of his mother's popcorn balls. He felt guilty, but Harper was too young for one anyway. She would just have to share hers with him this year. He knew once she got old enough to try one, she wouldn't be sharing hers with him again. Mama's popcorn balls were *that* good.

Peg and Larry's house was next. They answered the door dressed as Dagwood and Blondie and made quite the pair. Peg was known in the neighborhood for passing out full-size candy bars on Halloween in years past. Times had not changed. They received a full-size Snicker bar and a full-size Butterfinger in Harper's mini pumpkin bucket. Harper did not notice; however, Kendall and Anthony were stoked about the extra-large treats.

Next, they headed to Harry's house. He answered the door in his general's uniform. Kendall nearly fell backward when she saw him. Harry looked so distinguished and professional. She had never seen him so confident with better posture. He dropped several Hershey kisses into Harper's pumpkin and gave everyone real hugs and real kisses. He was enjoying his night because he was having non-stop visitors, which he loved.

Madge's house was next. Anthony and Mama both tried to prepare Kendall before they headed over to Madge's house, but nothing could have prepared Kendall for what actually happened. After they rang her doorbell, Madge quickly opened the door in her robe mumbling and muttering and then she dropped a travel-size toothbrush and a bar of soap into Harper's bucket. As Anthony saw them drop in, he thanked Madge and wished her a great night. Good thing because Kendall was totally speechless. Kendall could not imagine why she was so frustrated or why she might feel the need to give a nine-month-old child personal care products for Halloween, but then again maybe they made as much sense as giving a child a handful of candy.

Anthony said as they left her porch, "Don't worry! Madge will be Madge. We just probably interrupted her TV watching. She takes her prime-time dramas seriously, or so I have heard from my mom and her other friends, not that that explained the soap and toothbrush."

Their last stop was a bit of a stroll up the street and around the bend. They did not mind. They were enjoying the nice October night. It was fun to trick or treat like a family and spend the night making memories. At Tish's house, Harper and Kendall and Anthony each got baggies filled with two homemade pumpkin sugar cookies iced to perfection with Tish's yummy orange buttercream frosting. Tish was dressed in a nurse's uniform. She thought it was cute and suited her because she was, in fact, a nurse. Tish thought her cookies were the reason for the line outside her house that went down her driveway and down the sidewalk. Her cookies were quite the treat for sure. People loved her cookies that was true, but that night they were knocking on her door to get a glimpse of Tish in her costume, not to get cookies. Anthony and Kendall giggled all the way down the driveway thinking about her naïveté.

Once the three of them made it back to Kendall's, two of them had a hard time deciding what treat to try first. Anthony went for the popcorn ball, and Kendall opted for the iced pumpkin cookies. Kendall had her cup of milk and was as happy as a clam spending the evening with her new "parents."

Just as Kendall laid Harper down in her bed, she heard a siren coming from the front of her house. She was so frightened that someone had gotten hurt. She looked out the front window with Anthony and realized that a police car was parked directly in front of Madge's house.

Anthony immediately called his mom to get the scoop. He just knew she would know what was going on, and he was right.

"Mom, what is going on at Madge's?"

"Well, all I know is that I was on the porch passing out treats when I heard lots of yelling coming from her house. There was a family on her porch, and she was yelling obscenities and shaking her finger at the father of the group. The whole family was dressed in costume, in black, but I am not sure what they were dressed as. I'm not certain. I do not have all the facts yet, but if I were guessing, I would guess Madge was watching those dramas she loves so much, got up to answer the door, and then got spooked that they were there to rob her and steal those dad-gum coins. She probably got so involved in her shows that she forgot it was Halloween. I mean, you know Madge. It was bound to happen. God love her, but she can be a little off sometimes."

"That does sound possible. She seemed awfully frustrated when she answered her door for us, as well. We are glad it wasn't something more serious. Let us know if your guesses are correct when you get the whole scoop tomorrow, Mom. Love you, have a great rest of your night! Don't stay up too late handing out those balls! I will take any of your leftovers! You know I love those things!"

CHAPTER SEVENTEEN

November

N ovember turned out to be a tough month for most everyone in Kendall's life, including Kendall. Anthony loved
working outside of the city, but he was struggling to make connections for all the aspects of his business in the suburbs. He had
incredible connections in the city, however.

Reign had been working steadily at the gallery since returning
from her honeymoon, but she was down because she and Branton
moved into the house they loved, but it did not have a studio space
like Branton had wanted. He was making the space he had work
and definitely creating artwork, but he was frustrated and there

was friction between him and Reign, as a result. And Reign's short temper at work with Kendall was creating some tension, as well.

Kendall was struggling with juggling time at home with Harper, work, and time alone with Anthony. She was feeling stretched very thin and she wondered where things would break first. She had not seen the neighbors, besides Mama, since they all came over to meet Harper that first day at Kendall's and she was feeling guilty about that. She wanted to take time off to shop for the holidays, but she knew *that* was out of the question. One day after returning home from work, Kendall walked next door to Mama's to pick up Harper. Harper was asleep, so Mama made them both a cup of tea and made Kendall sit on the couch and chat. Mama was very intuitive, and she could tell Kendall was struggling even though Kendall had not dared to complain about a thing to anyone. Mama finally got her to talk. Kendall was tired, and Mama asked the right questions in such a way that Kendall's protective walls crashed down right in front of Mama and Kendall began to open up.

"Are you overwhelmed? Is the responsibility of Harper and a serious relationship a lot to manage? Is getting to the gallery each day getting harder and harder? Listen, I raised Anthony, and I helped a lot of my friends take care of their children. I am helping you out because I love you and Harper, and I will continue for as long as I need to. Please don't think twice about that!"

"It isn't just that. My priorities have really been shifting lately, really all year. Things just matter that didn't matter and things that used to be my whole world don't really matter much anymore. I love Anthony. I want to marry him one day, so I do not want to lose him over all this struggle with time management. My struggles in this area have caused me to have relationship problems in the past. Also, I can tell Reign is losing interest in the gallery. I really think she wants to get back into design. I have passed all the designers off to her and when I hear them talking during meetings in the gallery, Reign seems happier than I have ever seen her before. She has made some good designer friends. Her husband needs more studio space, and so he is very frustrated. I hate that she and her new husband are already having some issues. Also, Harper needs me more now than my gallery does, and I know that, but I am struggling with what that means for me and what I worked so hard to build. I now care more about being a great mom and partner than I do about being a successful business owner, and I certainly never thought I would say that this year or ever in my life, if I am honest."

"Well, Ken, you know me pretty well by now. Mama's got some words to say, but I'm not going to share them all. If I did, the decisions would be mine not yours. Harper is still asleep. You go home, get in a warm bath, and think about everything you just told me, and I know you will come up with the perfect solution for every situation you mentioned. You do not have problems. You have got a *life* and that, my dear, is a good thing. Our lives can get tricky sometimes. We must make choices to go down different roads that lead to different places when things do not seem to be working out as we know they could or as we would like. It is nice to have options. Be thankful for them. Trust your gut and follow it. Now, go on and listen to what your gut and your heart are telling you to do while you are in that bathtub. Your heart knows, and it will tell you! I promise! I have had a lifetime of doing just that, and it works every single time."

Kendall left Harper sleeping at Mama's and did just as she suggested. And she wasn't in the extra warm water five minutes before she started getting ideas. Everything was connected just like Mama had said. And Kendall thought of a plan that just might help everyone involved. Kendall finally got out of the bath after working through her plans, threw on mismatched comfy clothes, picked up Harper next door and was in a totally different mood by the time Anthony arrived at her house for dinner and a movie.

Kendall told Anthony she wanted him to drive into the gallery the next day to attend a meeting she was having at noon and to bring her mom and Harper too. Kendall texted Reign and Branton asking them to do the same. Well, Reign would already be at the gallery, but she asked her to have Branton come in to attend the meeting. Everyone was curious about why she would call a meeting, but Kendall knew they would find out soon enough.

After their movie was over and after they put Harper to bed, Kendall begged Anthony to stay the night, this time not to help with Harper, but because she did not want him to leave. She wanted him next to her all night long.

The next morning at the gallery Reign acted a bit strange. She was concerned about what Kendall's meeting was about, and it was messing with her head and her workday. Kendall could sense something was up, but she knew it would all be cleared up in just a few hours.

At 11:30, Mrs. Rashida Taylor walked in the door on her lunch break smiling and looking chipper. She knew Reign and Kendall would be shocked she was still working, but she loved her job. Rashida asked Reign if Kendall was around.

"She is in the office. Let me run let her know you are here," said Reign

Kendall rushed out of the office asking, "What brings you by? Have you been living the high life after the news?"

"Well, not really. I am just living my life just like I was. I liked it then, and I still like it. I have continued working. I am not too far from retiring, so I promised the partners I would stay on for the duration. The reason I came by today was to pay you for your help, Kendall. Without your help connecting me with Christie's, I would still have that painting leaning against the wall in the back of some closet. You, Kendall and Mr. Andrew Wyeth, are the reason I got paid at all. I was just shopping at that garage sale for planters for all my house plants. I wasn't ever looking to buy a painting. It just caught my eye, and now I'm glad it did. I wanted to drop off this envelope to show my appreciation."

Rashida handed a small white envelope to Kendall, thanked both Reign and Kendall for all their help, wished them a blessed day, and then in a flash exited the gallery to grab lunch with friends.

Kendall opened the envelope to find a note and a check for two million dollars. Kendall screamed and then started crying while reading the attached note out loud to Reign.

> *Dearest Kendall of Gallery 116,*
>
> *Without you, I would never have been paid a thing. This is for you to use as you see fit. I do not need the money I am sharing with you. I have no children to pass it down to. I already have a great job and the rest of the money will be more than I could use in my lifetime. Please know that I will be forever grateful for your kindness and your help. Please accept this in the spirit it was given.*
>
> *With love, Rashida*

Kendall looked up at Reign to tell her that Mrs. Taylor had given them a check for two million dollars, and then showed her the check and the note to read for herself. Reign was floored. She cried too. Kendall was stunned and thankful. The timing could not have been more perfect, and just in time for her noon meeting.

Just before noon, Mama and Anthony walked in the door pushing Harper in her pink animal print stroller, followed by Branton in his favorite blue jean overalls. Reign joined them all in the middle of the gallery. Anthony could tell that Kendall seemed different. Something was up. He was curious about what it was and why she had called a meeting with these specific people and no one else. Mama was excited! She knew! Mama knew! Mama always knows and always knows what's best! Anthony had told her so, and now Kendall was learning that truth for herself.

Kendall put the closed sign on the gallery door and started the meeting at 12 o'clock on the dot. She welcomed everyone and thanked them for driving into the gallery on such a beautiful, crisp fall day.

"First off, I want to thank you, Mama, for always being willing to watch Kendall whenever needed this past month. It has meant the world to me."

Kendall looked at Harper in her stroller and said, "Harper Honey, thank you for coming into my life. I know it was not your choice, but I am thankful every day for you. You have changed my life in the very best ways. You, my little hummingbird, are a precious real-life reminder to live every day to the fullest enjoying each and every precious moment."

Next, Kendall addressed Reign, "Reign, you have been my right hand, my loyal assistant for almost a year now. As promised, you have kept me organized and on task. And, you have become one of my best and dearest friends, but I have been concerned about you for a while. You seem stressed and short tempered here some days. It has caused me to wonder if our time here together has run its course. I have seen you interacting with all our designer clients. I saw how thrilled you were helping Anthony design and decorate the interior of his new home. And I know you are itching to get back into interior design—what you were trained to do."

"Branton, I see the stress in your eyes, and I know it is rubbing off on your marriage to Reign. I know you all have a new house you love, but no designated studio space to do your creating and you deserve one."

"Anthony, my Dear Anthony, love of my life, I know my energies are divided every which way these days. Lately, I've barely eked out time for us and that hasn't been fair. You have supported my bringing Harper into my life in every way possible, but that decision has put strain on our still rather new relationship and for that I am sorry. I know you moved out to the suburbs for us and moved your office for you and for us, but it has been hard for you to make connections out there. That burden has been weighing on me too. I feel partly to blame."

"Everyone just hang with me, ok? I am going somewhere with all of this." Harper squealed as Kendall finished speaking causing them all to giggle, and Kendall thought she heard Harper say, "Mama" for the first time and so did everyone else. "Was that what I thought it was?" Kendall asked.

"Yep! It sure was! We've been working on that. I thought I could accomplish a two for one deal on that one if I could get her to say it," said Mama. Kendall started to cry as Anthony looked at her and the others just laughed because they knew Mama was always up to something behind the scenes. She was a teacher and a helper down deep in her soul and everyone in the gallery for the meeting loved that about her.

Kendall continued, "That will do a number on a new mom, for sure. Well, that actually illustrates my point perfectly. Hear me out, everyone, before you speak. I do not want to miss a single moment like we just experienced, so I am going to close the gallery for good after our annual customer Christmas party. Branton, I want you to consider renting or purchasing the space. You could set up your studio here like you did while I was away earlier this year. You could call it the Branton Fleming Gallery and sell your work, exclusively. Reign, I want you to start your own interior design business on your own or with some of our designers whom you already know. And I think you should partner with Anthony, I mean, for *work only*, of course. He needs an interior design consult often, and you could be his connection in the suburbs since you and Branton live out there now. I am closing the gallery to stay home with Harper full time. Mama, that means you can babysit like a real grandmother, as needed, instead of like a nanny as you have been doing lately. I know you all are worried about how I could make all of this a possibility. Well, remember the painting that the lady found at the garage sale? Well, it sold at action for way more than expected, and Mrs. Rashida Taylor, the owner who put the painting up for auction, shared some of that money with me today. With that money, I want to pay Reign more than her salary for her time here with me, and I want to help her set up her own interior design firm. The rest of the money I will put away for me and Anthony and for Harper to ensure that I can always stay home and be her mom, first and foremost."

The group all ran to Kendall to give her hugs. They loved her ideas and thought they were perfect solutions to solve what had been concerning them all, and they thanked Kendall for sharing those solutions with the group. They also wanted to hear all about the auction and Mrs. Taylor's gift. Everyone was stunned, but thankful that Kendall loved them all enough to call the meeting and to share their burdens and to make suggestions to help solve their issues as best as she could. The bath had paid off. Mama looked over at Kendall and mouthed, "I told you so."

Anthony hugged Kendall and then pulled her back away from him and looked her directly in the eyes and said, "Today is a perfect example of why I love you! You are one special lady with a heart of gold." Anthony kissed her and said, "Let's call it a day! We can take Harper home, then we can take her for a walk around our neighborhood to look at the leaves, and then I can thank you for putting us first. How does that sound?"

CHAPTER EIGHTEEN

December

K endall and Reign left the first week of December for their trip to Miami for Art Basel. It was not a convenient time, but they had made their reservations earlier in the year and felt terrible about cancelling.

Kendall had always wanted to attend and now that she had Reign to travel with, she was quite excited. They had decided to make it a girls' trip. Anthony and Mama were taking care of Harper, and Branton was using the alone time to paint.

They had chosen to stay at the W. South Beach hotel since it was just an eleven-minute walk to the convention center. It was a pricey hotel, but convenience was key for this trip. They were going to be walking a ton. The galleries were open until seven each night. Kendall was most excited about spending time in the Positions Gallery. It was showcasing the work of emerging artists, and that was right up her alley. Kendall and Reign landed at two o'clock on the first day. They took an Uber straight to their hotel, checked in, and immediately walked to the convention center to get started viewing art and making connections. The connections on this trip would be for Reign and not Kendall, since Kendall was closing the gallery after the Christmas party. This was Reign's first time at such an event. She was stunned at the magnitude of the show and surprised by so many different types of art. Reign felt like they walked miles the first day. Kendall felt odd walking through the galleries because her time in the art world, at least for now, was coming to an end. It was turning into quite a bittersweet trip, at least in her mind. Walking through one of the main galleries, Kendall ran into an old professor of hers, Tom Lloyd of all people. She could not believe she even recognized him. She had not seen him since graduation. She introduced him to Reign. Kendall asked why he was there and how he was doing.

"Oh, I, *we* come every year, my wife and I, that is. She is around here somewhere. She likes art as much as I do. We make a trip out of coming here every year. It is nice to be in some warm weather this time of year. New Haven is cold at Christmas time, as you know. We come down here, stay in a hotel, tour the show, walk on the beach and do some Florida Christmas shopping. Why are you ladies here?"

"Well," said Kendall. "I own a gallery now. Well, I do now, but after many successful years, I am closing it. We made plans to visit before my decision and Reign here is opening her very own design firm, so we decided to attend the show to help her see what the show has to offer and to help her make necessary connections that could potentially come in handy."

"Well, that all sounds good, but if your gallery is doing well, why close it?" Mr. Lloyd asked curiously.

"I recently got custody of my best friend's child after she passed away in an accident. I am in the process of adopting her officially this month. I guess the easiest way to say it is that my priorities have shifted. I have a very serious boyfriend too. We are talking about marriage. I want to be focused on both of them rather than be distracted and divided trying to earn a living and trying to become some version of what I had previously thought a successful person should be. My daughter has quickly become the center of my life where my gallery used to be."

"I totally understand! My wife and I have three grown daughters. They are still in the center of our world, but now joined by husbands and grandchildren. It all changes, but it also gets better and better. Trust me. Well, you ladies, enjoy your stay here! It was so great to run into you, Kendall! You have always been one of my favorite students. I remember how much you knew about art and your writing was so impressive to top it off. Reading your papers was such a joy. I can still remember them. Please enjoy your trip and take care!"

"You too! Professor Lloyd, it was great running into you! You and your wife enjoy your time here too!" Kendall hugged him and watched him walk off to meet up with his wife.

Right at seven o'clock, as the exhibition doors closed, Kendall and Reign headed back to the hotel.

"My dogs are barking," said Reign. "I think I'm going to soak my feet before we get dinner."

"I'm going to try to get a little nap in before dinner," said Kendall.

So, they headed into their room, each going their separate ways. Kendall fell onto the bed and was out like a light. She was awoken about an hour later by the ringing of her phone. She quickly answered.

"Ken, its Anthony. I do not mean to bother you. I know it is your first day away, but Harper is sick. She has been crying since she woke up from her nap."

Kendall's heart began racing as she asked, "What in the world? Have you called Tish or the doctor?"

"Yes, we did. She has been here for several hours. She has also been in constant contact with Harper's doctor. Harper is warm and pulling on her ears. Tish says to give her Tylenol and to get her in to be seen by her doc in the morning. She assured us that it could be a rough night with little or no sleep for any of us. Do not worry though, we have got this. Harper is in good hands. I just wanted to let you know. We all love you and I am sorry to bother you on your trip, but I knew you would want to know."

"Oh yes, I did! Thank you so much for calling! Please Tell Mama and Tish how much I appreciate what they are doing to help you out with this. Please keep me updated!"

Kendall got off the phone to share with Reign about what was going on.

"Oh, I hate to hear that! Let them oversee the appointment in the morning. We can go back to the show first thing to see a bit more, and then we can catch an earlier flight home."

"Earlier? You mean two days early? I hate to do that to you, Reign, but I do feel like I need to be home with Harper. Anthony is still trying to work. It isn't good or kind for me to expect him or Mama to stay up all night and to be dealing with this alone, without me. Harper is officially my responsibility. I hate that I'm away the first time she gets sick. It breaks my heart."

"It happens, Ken! It does not make you a bad mom.! She will get medicine in the morning, and we will be home before she eats dinner tomorrow night. Anthony is getting practice. Remember he is going to officially be her dad very soon. It is good for him to step up, and it is good for you to see that he is capable of doing so. He is, and he will be a great dad and Mama is going to be one special grandmother."

"Ok, I feel better now with a plan. I am starving though. May we please go get some food? I don't even care if we stay in the hotel."

"I'm up for the least amount of walking. That sounds perfect to me! The food I had at lunch is long gone." The girls headed down to the hotel restaurant to have dinner. It ended up being a very nice meal, and afterwards they were full and ready for bed. On the way back up to the room, Anthony called to let Kendall know that the Tylenol helped, and that Kendall had easily fallen off to sleep. Her hours of crying earlier in the evening, along with the medicine, had tired her out.

"We have an appointment at 9:30 in the morning. I will call you as soon as it is over."

Kendall thanked Anthony with tears in her eyes and let him know that they had changed their tickets, and that they would be home the next evening. He hated for them to have to change plans, but he was looking forward to Kendall being home and he knew Harper would be too. Kendall also assured Anthony that Reign had made connections that had made even the short trip worth it.

After sleeping well themselves, Kendall and Reign were up early. They had a nice breakfast at the hotel, then they arrived at the convention center just as the doors opened. They were able to make their way through a few more galleries. Reign chatted with many dealers and filled her purse with business cards and gallery brochures. Reign was really getting the hang of things. She was amazed by the huge and varied selection of art. Anthony called fifteen minutes after the appointment time to report that Harper had a double ear infection and a slight case of bronchitis. The doctor gave her medicine he had assured them would make her feel better before Kendall even got home. Kendall thanked Anthony for all his help. She knew he was going to make a great dad because he was already acting the part. Kendall was thankful, but ready to see her girl. She and Reign headed to the airport at two o'clock. If everything remained on schedule, she would be home with Anthony and Harper by six o'clock.

When Kendall finally walked in the door at 6:05, Harper let out a huge squeal. She seemed ecstatic to see her mother. Anthony and Mama greeted her each with a hug and a kiss. They too were surely happy to have her home.

Harper was already in her highchair waiting for her dinner. She held up her arms as Kendall walked over and Harper said, "Mama! Mama!" That melted Kendall's heart. She kissed Harper on the head, washed her hands and started feeding her the dinner the other momma had prepared. Kendall was exactly where she wanted to be—in her own cozy home with her little family. Miami had been fun, but that world wasn't for her anymore. The people now in her kitchen made that abundantly clear. They were her world now, and she could not be happier about it.

Kendall had spent the first few days back in the gallery after their trip to Miami planning the Christmas party for the 15th. Branton had officially confirmed his decision to rent the gallery space after her by signing the lease, so plans for that were also underway. Reign was still scheduled to work every day at the gallery up until the day of the party. She had been hard at work writing up her business plans though, connecting with designers and looking for her own office space. Kendall had broken the news of the gallery's closing to all of her other artists. None of them seemed disappointed or upset, however. Inglewood had many other gallery connections he was pursuing. Susie was fine with not having a gallery. She had been painting less after her grandson's arrival anyway. Leslie was far too busy with her own children to worry about the closing. She mentioned that she might just sell her work through her own website. Trixie even seemed fine to stick with New York City based galleries exclusively. She assured Kendall that in the end it would save her in shipping costs which would be helpful for her bottom line. Branton was looking forward to having the space, his own space. He had dropped by a few times to measure some spaces, to take pictures and to dream in person about his plans. Kendall could tell he was going to make very good use of the space. She was excited that her customers would know exactly where to continue to see and to purchase his work.

Kendall's planning for the Christmas party was not unlike the spring art show. She had contacted the caterers again and ordered invitations and flowers to go along with her traditional holiday gallery decorations.

Kendall's father was flying in on the 20th to spend Christmas with everyone, so he would not be in town for the party. He was sad to be missing Kendall's last big gallery event, but he had missed many in the past before. He would be in town on the 22nd, however, just in time for the final court hearing. This one was to finalize Harper's adoption. Mr. Gardener had been able to pull some strings to speed things up for Kendall, making the finalizing just in time for Christmas.

With the Christmas gallery party, Harper's first birthday party, her father's visit, and Christmas swiftly approaching, Kendall was trying to squeeze in time to go Christmas shopping. She had more on her list to shop for this year than last year, and it too was going to take planning and time to accomplish.

Kendall had just realized after daydreaming at her desk about all the events on the horizon that she needed to call Harry to check up on him and to see if he was a grandfather yet. If she had remembered the timing correctly, it should be just about time for Cora's baby to be born. Kendall knew she must call immediately, or she would forget, so she dialed his number straight away.

"Hello, this is Harry. Who is this?"

"Harry, this is Kendall Fitzpatrick. I am calling from work to check in on you. It has been a while. Are you getting ready for Christmas?" Kendall asked curiously.

"I sure am, and *I* have a new grandbaby— born two days ago. Can you believe it? Named him after me and everything. I'm just tickled blue. His name is Benjamin Harold Albright. What ya think of that? Pretty special, huh?" Harry asked proudly.

"Cora and her new husband are going to bring him here for a visit at Christmas. They finally got married. Isn't that the best? I'm so excited I can hardly stand it."

Kendall got off the phone with Harry after promising to drop by his house to see pictures on his computer sometime soon. She wrote that down in her planner before she forgot, then stood up from her computer to go check on Reign. She hadn't seen her come into the office in a while.

Kendall walked out front and did not see Reign. She went back to the office to make sure she hadn't overlooked her sitting at her desk, but no Reign.

Kendall began shouting, "Reign? Reign, where *are* you?"

However, Kendall heard no reply. She started to get really concerned although she had not heard the bell on the front door ring all afternoon, so she knew Reign had to still be in the gallery somewhere. Kendall went back into the office to call Reign on her cell phone.

"Hello." Reign answered.

"Where are you?" Kendall asked concerned.

"I am in the bathroom. Where else would I be?"

I am not sure. I just haven't seen you for a bit, and it had me worried."

"Well, maybe you should be. I feel terrible! My stomach hasn't been right since I ate that Indian food at noon. I knew I should have had a salad like I have every day for lunch!"

"Well, *I* feel fine, and we ate the same thing. I will be in there in just a second to check on you."

Kendall walked into the bathroom as Reign was splashing water on her face. Reign was white as a ghost. Reign said she had thrown up *multiple* times. "You go back into the office and sit down. I will get you a Sprite. Do you want me to call Branton to come get you? If you can wait just a little bit, I can drive you home when I leave. That way we don't have to bother Branton."

"I sure hope you don't get this bug and pass it to Harper and Anthony. I would hate for that to happen.

"Not a chance, Reign! You don't have a bug, Dear!"

"How do you know? I feel horrible and it is the exact time of year when people get the stomach bug."

"I don't doubt you feel terrible, but I'm not gonna catch anything. Think about it, Reign! You are pregnant!"

"You are hilarious! No way! Not me, not *now*!"

"Well, I hate to tell you, Girl, but that is usually how it works. The timing isn't always how you plan it. I haven't been pregnant before. Therefore, I'm no expert, but I can help you make room if you are."

Kendall eventually drove Reign home, stopping by the drugstore on the way to pick up a pregnancy test for Reign. Reign wanted to take the test before she broke the news to Branton. She knew he would be surprised, but thrilled. She knew in her heart that Kendall was correct now that she thought about it, but she needed the lines to confirm it.

As Reign got out of the car, Kendall said, "I may have been wrong. My stomach *is* really starting to *hurt*. I am not feeling good *at all*. I'm probably *getting it*."

"*See*, I told you Kendall! It's a *bug* or worse! Maybe we were *Poisoned*!"

Kendall leaned over the passenger seat to look at Reign after she had exited the car laughing hysterically and saying, "I'm totally kidding, Reign! I feel fine! Call me with the good news after you take the test and after you tell Branton!"

Kendall barely got in the door as Reign called. Kendall quickly answered dropping her things off on the hall table, "Hello. This is Kendall."

"Well, you were right! I am pregnant! I took the test and already told Branton. He is beside himself excited. I'm shocked. It is going to take me time to adjust. I've been planning my new business adventure. What will I do now?"

"You will take it all one step at a time and one day at a time. That is what you will do! Don't get ahead of yourself! It is a true blessing! You can work while pregnant if you want. You will find answers as you put one foot in front of the other. At least you and Branton are doing better. He is much happier planning the gallery. Ya'll will work through it all. Be excited! Please, don't get ahead of yourself! Speaking of not getting ahead of yourself or ourselves, Harper and your baby could be friends one day. I'm excited about that! Take the day off tomorrow and rest, but don't forget about Harper's party on Saturday!" Kendall said as she got off the phone to go inside to check on Harper and Mama.

When Kendall walked into Mama's front room, she happened upon a heartwarming scene. Mama was swinging Harper in her swing and singing nursery rhymes and children's songs while the smell of freshly baked chocolate chip cookies drifted through the air. Mama was just finishing up "William Matrimmatoe" as Kendall walked into Mama's family room.

After picking up Harper, Kendall decided to take Harper over to Harry's house for a quick visit before dinner. She did not want to put off a visit with him any longer. She needed to see those cute new baby pictures. She also wanted to ask while she was there if he needed any help putting up Christmas decorations before Cora's visit.

On Saturday morning Anthony and Kendall were up early decorating for Harper's first birthday party that started at one o'clock. Tish had baked and decorated a three-tier cake with a big white "1" on the top, and Kendall purchased mini plastic farm animals that she also placed on top. The theme for the party was "One on the Farm" because Harper really loved practicing her animal sounds. Everyone was asked to dress in overalls or jeans like farmers on a farm. Kendall had decorated everywhere with farm animals of all types from cutouts to stuffed animals. Her front porch was decorated like a barn and Cola and Fendy were all set to play their parts as real-life animal decorations. Anthony was planning to cook hotdogs and hamburgers on the grill. Kendall cut up fresh fruit and made a big green salad to go with the meal. All the neighbors were bringing their choice of beverage. Kendall had her camera ready to capture all the special moments to share with her father since he couldn't be there. The Connors were expected to celebrate, however. Kendall assumed it would be a hard day for them, but she thought they would want to be there. Reign was feeling a bit better, so she was bringing Branton. Branton was excited to not feel guilty for once about wearing his favorite overalls. The decorating had taken most of the morning while also taking care of Harper. Harper was taking her first steps and liked to be independent, but still required much supervision. Anthony took over Harper duty so Kendall could grab a shower and get ready. Kendall wanted to be available to greet the guests holding Harper decked out in her mini overalls and cowboy hat as all the guests arrived.

When guests arrived, Harper acted like she knew they were there for her. She smiled and waved at each visitor. She loved all the decorations, and so did the guests. Harper received more gifts than she needed, but they were all appreciated. Her favorite seemed to be a brown teddy bear from Harry. Harper loved the cake Tish made. She showed her appreciation by diving into it headfirst. She was sitting in her highchair as Kendall held onto the cake as she ate her first bite. She enthusiastically poked her whole face into the side of the cake and covered her face with icing. She had not ever had *that* much sugar, and it showed. She loved every bit she got. She had icing from head to toe, and she was licking her fingers clean as Kendall took the cake away and then picked Harper up out of her highchair. Harper rotated from guest to guest during the entire party. She was not shy nor picky. She seemed to love everyone, and they loved her too. She spent time opening and playing with her new toys in front of the crowd, but then she finally walked over to Kendall with her bear and pointed to her room. She liked her naps, and that day was no different. Kendall picked her up, let Harper wave goodbye to all her guests, and then Kendall took her back to her room for a nap. All the guests visited for a few more minutes and then headed home, some even heading home to have a nap themselves.

As the last guest left, Kendall looked at Anthony and her living room floor covered in toys, bags and wrapping paper and said, "What a day! I think it was very special. Harper had such fun with her grandparents and all the neighbors. I cannot believe we pulled off her first of many birthday parties. Cola and Fendy played their parts like pros." Kendall said bending down to pick up paper off the floor.

Then, she walked to the kitchen to throw the paper away. As she walked back into the living room, Anthony was down on one knee. Kendall assumed he too was cleaning up, but she was wrong.

Anthony said, "Come here! I've got something to ask you! You know you are the love of my life. We aren't on some mountain top, but we are. It looks a little different for us. I wouldn't want to ask you to be my wife any other place after doing anything other than what we have done today. This is our life—yours mine, and Harper's. Will you make me the happiest man around and marry me, Ken?" Anthony asked, putting a ring on her finger. "I love you and Harper with all of my heart!"

"Oh Anthony, you surprised me! I had no idea! This ring is beautiful! I love you so much, and of course I will marry you! Call your mom and tell her to come over quickly! Don't tell her why! We could run over there, but Harper is asleep, and I want to surprise Mama!"

Anthony's mom came bounding in the door five minutes later. Anthony and Kendall were casually sitting on the couch acting as though nothing had happened when she ran into the living room.

"What is wrong? Why did you call and make me rush over here? Ya'll are just sitting on the couch in the middle of this party mess. You don't expect me to clean up for you, do you?"

"Well, we are too tired to move. Could you please hand us the remote?" Kendall asked pointing toward the remote with her left hand wiggling it in the process.

Mama just looked at them both frustrated and disgusted. "Oh, come on guys! Really?" Kendall continued holding up, pointing and wiggling her hand and Mama just continued to stare. It was a weird moment in time where time seemed to stand still. Finally, Mama noticed the ring and started screaming. She figured it out. They weren't tired or lazy, and they didn't want the remote either. They had just gotten engaged, and they wanted to let her know in a way Mama would remember and appreciate.

Mama said, "Congratulations you two! It is about time!" And with that, Harper started crying and woke up from her nap. Mama had been a little too enthusiastic with her screaming which woke the baby. No one worried about that, however, because actually all three of them wanted to celebrate with Harper anyway. Kendall went to get Harper up and to tell her the big news along with her father, Reign and Branton and all of the neighbors if she could beat Mama to it, that is. Mama was just as excited as Kendall and Anthony were. Mama was finally, officially, going to have a daughter and a granddaughter after many years, and she was thrilled to announce it to anyone willing to listen.

Kendall and Anthony spent the next day helping Harry retrieve all of his Christmas decorations from his attic. They had not been touched in years and there was enough dust on each box to prove it. They even drove Harry to pick out a real tree at a Christmas tree farm, which was per his request.

"I can't thank you two enough! Mildred always had us use a nasty old fake tree. I prefer real ones! The smell of pine reminds me of chopping down our family tree with my father when I was a kid."

On the way home, they stopped by the hardware store to get a tree stand for his live tree. He already had plenty of working lights and ornaments. They knew that because they had all meticulously checked each strand before heading out to get the tree.

When they got back to the house, Anthony made a fire for Harry and Kendall made them all hot cocoa. She added sweet foam to the top and peppermint sticks for garnish, all things she had brought over from her house. They spent the afternoon decorating Harry's tree and chatting together. Kendall had helped get out some of Mildred's favorite decorations like her caroler collection Harry said she used to place on the piano and her white ceramic nativity that she always placed on a white piece of felt on the buffet table in their dining room. Kendall helped Harry place everything just so. Then, Harry asked Anthony to get one last thing down from a high shelf in the back of the garage--Santa's sleigh that he had always placed in the yard at Christmas as Cora was growing up. They also discovered the original spotlight he had used to highlight that sleigh. Harry had Anthony help him set it up for Cora. The sleigh had always been her favorite seasonal decoration. Harry knew she was going to love seeing it lit up in the yard as she arrived for her holiday visit.

Harry was going all out with Kendall and Anthony's help because he was excited that he had a new grandbaby to celebrate

Christmas with and most of all, Cora was coming home to celebrate for the first time in years and bringing her new husband
and the baby. Cora and her husband had gotten married at their
courthouse to make their union official, which pleased Harry immensely. He had shared the news proudly with Kendall again and
with Anthony during their day together. Harry thanked Kendall
and Anthony over and over for the help and the company. He also
assured them that Mildred would have approved of their accom-
plishments. Anthony and Kendall and Harper headed home just
after five to have dinner and relax before a busy workday the next
day.

The gallery Christmas party to celebrate Christmas had turned
into a party to celebrate the success of Gallery 116 and Kendall and
Anthony's engagement too. It had turned into a multi-purpose
event. Reign and Kendall decorated for Christmas as Kendall had
done each year before. The caterer delivered food and the florist
dropped off poinsettias to place throughout the gallery. The scene
she and Reign had set was cozy, beautiful and festive. The gallery
looked and smelled like celebration and Christmas. "It is going to
be a night to remember," Kendall thought as she plugged in the
lights on the gallery tree for the *last* time.

All her favorite customers and clients showed up to celebrate
and to congratulate Kendall and Anthony. It was not hard to spot
the huge ring on Kendall's finger as she animatedly chatted with
all her guests in her emerald green, velvet dress that just happened
to match her green eyes perfectly. All of Kendall's local artists
gladly showed up to celebrate with her and to thank her for selling
their work through the years. Kendall was especially glad to see
Inglewood. He introduced Kendall to his new girlfriend, Grace,

who was visiting from South Florida. Inglewood had met her on his recent travels. Susie also attended with Joe, and she made sure to share photos of her new grandson with Kendall.

Rashida Taylor and her husband, Quincy, showed up to celebrate too. Rashida was so proud to introduce Quincy to Kendall. Arthur thanked Kendall for all her help with selling the painting. Kendall thanked Arthur for sharing some of the sale price with her.

"That was all Rashida. She is that kind of lady--generous, thankful and kind," he said. "That is why I love her so." Quincy said, putting his arm around his wife and kissing her on top of the head.

Some of Reign's designer friends showed up to celebrate too even though Reign had decided to open her business on her own. Reign had decided to name her new business "Reign Gardener Interiors." Her designer friends had given her suggestions about what samples to have on hand and what companies with which she should partner. Reign was proceeding with her plans in addition to being pregnant. She was that kind of strong, confident woman. Anthony was excited to be able to refer some of his clients to her. Reign was talented, and Anthony knew she could manage whatever he threw her way.

Kendall could not help but admire Reign's belly. The dress she wore was one that accentuated her pregnant belly. Kendall even went up to her once during the evening asking if she could touch her belly to feel the baby kick. They were those kinds of friends these days. Kendall tried to get Reign or Branton to spill the beans on what they were having, but they weren't caving. Kendall and

Anthony had an ongoing bet as to whether the two were having a boy or a girl.

Christmas carols were playing on the gallery speakers. It was snowing outside, and Kendall could see the snow falling under the streetlights as she looked outside. She looked around the room at the crowd of people and the impressive art on the walls, listened to the music and the excited chatter, saw the snow falling outside, and she started to cry. This gallery, her gallery, had been a success while it was open. And the people standing around the room had made it possible.

Anthony saw her standing alone scanning the room and brought her a glass of champagne saying, "Make a toast! These people deserve one!"

Kendall did make a toast to Reign, to her artists, and to her customers and clients. Reign made one to Kendall congratulating her on her engagement and on the success of the gallery and then Branton toasted to Kendall and to the gallery and thanked her for the years of support and encouragement. All the guests cheered and clapped and hugged Anthony and Kendall.

Kendall spent the rest of the evening by the door thanking all her guests for supporting her and for celebrating with her and wishing them all a Merry Christmas.

As the last guest left, Kendall hung the closed sign and turned toward Reign and Branton and Anthony, took off her shoes and said, "Merry Christmas! That's all folks! Thanks for a great night! I love you all! Let's head home to the burbs in the snow. I want to go home to see my girls!"

Kendall officially closed the gallery that night. That meant she had lots of free time until Christmas, which also meant she would have time to get shopping and wrapping completed before her father was due for a visit in five days. Kendall was also going to focus on decorating her house now that the gallery was closed, and the party was over. She had never had a Christmas tree with a one-year-old child before, but she did have one with a cat in the past and she figured it couldn't be that much worse and it probably wouldn't be that much better. Either way she was going to have to be on guard around the tree once she completed the decorating.

Kendall did devote one entire day off at home to decorating the real tree she and Anthony had purchased for her home at the local Christmas tree lot owned and operated by a local Boy Scout troop. She strung the lights alone because she was very particular about how they were done, and she did not want to have her first argument with Anthony over string lights. Kendall believed that ornaments should have special meaning and personal stories if they were to be hung on her tree. She despised perfectly decorated, impersonal, artificial trees decorated with color matching balls, themed ornaments and enormous decorative ribbon. Kendal preferred imperfect *real* Christmas trees with stories and personality and hers had both, and she loved it that way.

It was like going down memory lane when she decorated her tree, so she fixed a mug of hot cocoa, built a fire, turned on the Hallmark Channel, and made a day of it while remaining in her PJs the entire time. She took her time unwrapping the tissue of protection around each little treasure to carefully hang each precious ornament on just the right branch securing those that

needed a bit of extra support. All the ladies in the neighborhood
had given Kendall ornaments for Harper. Kendall waited until
Harper was up from her nap to hang those on the tree, so Harper
could assist or at least watch. All the artists from the gallery had
hand painted ornaments in their own style as gifts for Kendall,
which she cherished and so proudly hung on the tree. Kendall
then hung her own hummingbird ornament made from one of
her very own watercolor paintings. She had the tradition of making or ordering one very special Christmas ornament each year
to add to her collection. This year she used a photo of that small
watercolor she painted of a hummingbird to create her ornament.
Her hummingbird ornament was both delicate and fragile, made
of porcelain and it hung on a branch with a green silk ribbon.
She created it and hung it on their tree to remind her of the
hummingbirds that visit her yard each summer and to remind her
to slow down and to enjoy the precious present moments in life.
Reign had given Kendall two ornaments, one that looked like a
champagne flute to celebrate the year they had shared together and
one that looked like a designer purse to acknowledge their mutual
love of all things fashion, so she hung those next. Then, Anthony
had given Kendall an ornament from the mountain town where
they spent their weekend celebrating their birthdays, so she hung
it. Kendall's very favorite ornament of the year, however, was one
that Mama had made with Harper when she was keeping her one
day while Kendall was at work. It was a round ornament with
Harper's footprint on it. It had a tag attached to it saying, "Thank
you for letting me walk into your life! Love, Harper!" Kendall
had saved the best for last and placed that final ornament on their
tree. She stood back and admired it. She then changed out of her

pajamas, gathered up her things and Harper, and headed over to Anthony's to do the same thing at his house while he was away at work. She planned to put the lights on his tree and to hang a few of his ornaments to get started and then save some new ones for him to place on the tree after he returned home from work. If she didn't get the process started, she knew he would not have a decorated tree at all this year. He spent most of his waking hours not at work, but at her home anyway. However, she wanted his front window to have Christmas lights on and shining brightly for him to see when he pulled into the driveway as a surprise. It was the least she could do with her free day at home away from the gallery. Harper seemed to enjoy the lights and the decorating. She was acting like it, anyway, smiling and giggling and talking gibberish to Cola and Kendall. She had almost mastered Cola's name as she had "Mama". Kendall hoped "Dada" would be next.

Kendall spent the rest of the night, after decorating both trees, addressing Christmas cards. She had not sent cards for many years. Why would she have? She never thought she had anything to announce or anyone to send cards to and she preferred sharing wishes for a Merry Christmas or for Happy Holidays in person. This year she was sending a card with a picture taken of her, Harper and Anthony during one of the first hearings. She had a long list of clients and friends to wish a Merry Christmas and lots of news to share, as well. She signed each card with joy and thankfulness in her heart and with a smile on her face.

Kendall's father arrived on the 20th, but this time Harper, Anthony *and* Mama rode with her to the airport to pick him up. Everyone was glad to have him back in town to celebrate

Christmas with them. They all laughed and teased him because he brought one whole extra suitcase just for gifts.

He explained by saying, "I have a granddaughter now! Geez! I have an excuse! Don't tease me!"

Kendall and Anthony knew it wasn't just a bag full of gifts for Harper, but a suitcase full of gifts for Harper and Mama too, but again, they weren't mad about it.

As they drove into Kendall's driveway after picking up Arthur at the airport, Kendall noticed that the Greenberg turkey had been delivered and that it was on the porch in its box. Greenberg turkeys are specialty smoked turkeys shipped directly from Tyler, Texas, and one of Kendall's favorite December family traditions. She orders hers each year to be delivered on one of her busiest days of the season to make preparing dinner on those evenings simple and easy and super yummy. One of Kendall's all-time favorite Christmas activities growing up was picking up the box after one of the turkeys had been delivered and putting her nose up to the holes in the box to get a whiff of that smoky aroma. To Kendall, it never seemed like Christmastime until the Greenberg turkey arrived. There was nothing that smelled more like Christmas to her than the smell of that smoked turkey. Just smelling it made her mouth water. After removing the box from the porch, Kendall sniffed the holes and quickly took the box inside and sliced the turkey like a professional turkey carver. She was planning to serve the turkey with rolls, pickles and cranberries to make the best little sandwiches for their dinner that night. Kendall could tell her father was thrilled by the smile on his face as he watched her bring the box inside. Kendall did not know how long it had been since he and her mom had ordered one. Kendall had grown up eating one every year during the holidays, and her parents always made sure to order *her* one each year after she left home though. She could hardly wait to share the turkey and the tradition with Anthony and his mom. She knew they were going to love it. She was planning to have the delicious smoked turkey sandwiches with her seasonal specialty peppermint milkshakes while they watched *White Christmas*. It was one of her father's favorite movies of all time, not just his favorite Christmas movie, and it was going to be fun watching it and eating some of her favorite goodies with some of her favorite people. She was so glad to have her dad back in town to celebrate with everyone for what was sure to be an exciting week.

Two days after Arthur's arrival, Kendall along with Anthony and Harper had to appear in court before a judge for the hearing on the case for Kendall's official adoption of Harper. What Anthony and Kendall had not shared with anyone was the fact that Mr. Gardener had been able to include Anthony's name on the paperwork which would make Anthony's paperwork to adopt Harper much quicker once they were officially married. So, in a way Kendall and Anthony were both adopting Harper at the hearing.

There was a small audience in the courtroom that morning to support Kendall and Anthony and Harper—the Conners, Reign and Branton, Arthur, Mr. Gardener, Mama and even Harry. Kendall had dressed Harper in a plaid Christmas dress with red tights and tiny little Mary Jane black patent leather shoes. The small crowd stood as the judge entered the courtroom. Anthony, Kendall and Harper walked to the front of the room as the group sat down. They were sworn in, and then they answered questions under oath. The judge seemed to be in some kind of hurry. Maybe he too was excited for Christmas! After shuffling through papers, he announced that on the twenty-second day of December he was awarding custody of Harper Ruth McCollum to Ms. Kendall Fitzpatrick and eventually to Mr. Anthony Leone after his up-coming marriage to Ms. Kendall Fitzpatrick at the end of January. The judge signed the order and the request to have Harper's nam e officially changed to Harper Ruth McCollum Fitzpatrick. The crowd all clapped and dried their eyes. Everyone was surprised Anthony had been part of the ruling and excited that they were getting married as soon as the end of January which would finally make their little family official. By the first of February, both Kendall and Harper would have to change their names. Harper's name would have to be changed again, and Kendall would change hers and Harper's to Leone for good.

Kendall was excited to spend Christmas in her little house with her father, Mama, Anthony and Harper. Gifts were both overflowing and packed tightly underneath the tree. Mama and Kendall had already placed their homemade cut-out sugar cookies along with a carrot for Rudolph on a plate in front of the fireplace. They wanted to make memories and start traditions as early as possible with Harper. Their hand knitted stockings were hanging on the mantel. Carolers had just come to the door singing "Joy to the World" and Arthur and Anthony were whispering about the gifts they had purchased. Harper was busy playing with her kid-friendly nativity set when everyone was suddenly startled by the sound of the doorbell. Kendall got up to answer the door to find Harry dressed as Santa holding his darling grandson.

"Hello all! Merry Christmas! I just wanted to drop by and introduce you to my new grandson, Benjamin. Cora persuaded me to pull this costume out of the attic, and I had to show it and this little guy off to my neighbor friends on this lovely Christmas Eve. Isn't he cute?"

Kendall invited him in and quickly introduced Harper to Benjamin. After Harry left to take Benjamin back to Cora and her husband, Kendall took pictures of Harper with Santa's plate of cookies and with Harper and her stocking. Mama took a few photos of Kendall, Anthony and Harper and both girls and Arthur before Kendall put Harper to bed. Harper needed a good night's rest because the next day was sure to be a busy one. It would be Harper's second Christmas, but her *first* Christmas with her *new* family. After Harper went to bed, Arthur and Mama went over to her house to sleep. Their plan was to come over early the next morning for a breakfast of orange rolls and coffee before opening the presents. After they left, Kendall and Anthony began the real parenting duties of putting together Santa's toys that needed assembling. The task took three hours. Luckily, they watched *The Holiday* while they read instructions to help pass the time. This year they learned the hard way. Next year they would read the instructions a few days sooner. They were finally able to crawl into bed just before midnight. Anthony was sleeping over again because he did not want to miss a thing on Christmas morning, at least that was what he and Kendall were telling themselves.

Anthony woke up bright and early on Christmas morning, turned on the tree lights, and started a fire in the fireplace and a pot of coffee in the kitchen just in time to welcome Mama and Arthur as they entered the back door. Kendall and Harper were not even up yet. Anthony and Kendall had already decided to let the baby determine the schedule, just for the day. However, Anthony had no interest in waking either girl before they were ready, but the tree was lit, and it smelled like the makings of a perfect Christmas Day whenever the girls did decide to get out of bed.

Harper slept until eight as did Kendall. Kendall woke up rested, thankful and ready for the day ahead. After eating orange rolls, the crew checked out what they each received in their stockings, and then moved to the living room around the tree to unwrap presents. Anthony gave Cola the bone she got in her stocking to keep her happy and Kendall let Harper open her gifts first, so she would stay occupied throughout the morning, just like Cola. Harper had fun with all the paper and boxes, but her favorite gifts were her toy phone and a new baby doll with brown hair just like hers. Mama had sewn homemade custom doll clothes for Harper's new babydoll, and she had Madge knit the babydoll her very own blanket that matched the one Madge had made for Harper when she first came home to live with Kendall.

Kendall's first gift to open was from her father, and it was an Erin Condren planner just like the ones he had given her in previous years. Kendall thanked him knowing that *this* planner would be filled with different things, fewer things, simpler things than before--fewer meetings and far more joy.

Anthony then opened a gift from Kendall, an Hermès cashmere sweater. He tried it on immediately. It fit well, and he loved it. Mama received a new red notebook with stone paper and a few new pens from Kendall so she could write down her recipes with ease and have fun doing it. Next, Anthony brought in a wrapped box from Kendall's bedroom. The box wiggled as he put it in Mama's lap. She began to remove the wrapping paper as Cola and Fendy jumped on the couch with her, both curious and concerned.

Mama was confused as to why the animals were so nosey until out of the box climbed the cutest little black kitten. Mama squealed with delight just like a child.

"You guys shouldn't have, but I'm so glad you did! My very own Fendy, but I'm naming mine "Licorice." Isn't that a perfect name? I have wanted a black cat named Licorice since I was eight years old. I read a story about a black kitten then and wanted one of my own. How could you both know? You couldn't know. I have never told a soul, not even your father, Anthony. Thank you both so much! This little guy is going to keep me company when everyone else is busy."

Next, Kendall and Anthony gave her father his gift, a plane ticket to come back to the wedding in a month. Arthur was very thankful and so looking forward to his next visit already.

Kendall opened one of her gifts from Anthony next. It was a coffee table book about Greece. Kendall was confused as she flipped through the obviously beautiful book until she saw the reservation printout for the hotel and plane ticket information folded and tucked inside. She realized that those were their tickets and the dates coordinated with their honeymoon dates. She was over the moon. "What a way to share the news! How fun! I cannot wait to go there with you," she said looking at Anthony.

Arthur gave Anthony a first-edition antique architecture book. He gave Lucille (he preferred to call her that) a large pasta serving bowl made by a Phoenix potter. And he also gave Kendall a pair of her mother's favorite diamond earrings that he knew Kendall had always admired. He gave Harper her first very own mini pearl bracelet meant for the arm of a babe that he had picked out at a jewelry store back home.

Arthur had loved his Christmas with Kendall, Harper and the Leones. He especially loved shopping for everyone. It had given him hope again. And Kendall loved having him join her in the life and family she was building. She was sad they had missed so many Christmases together, but she wasn't living in the past anymore. There was too much joy in the present to waste time back there.

Arthur had spent the days before Christmas visiting Kendall and celebrating the adoption, and then they celebrated Christmas together. It had been a busy five days since he had arrived, but he wasn't quite ready to head home alone just yet. He asked Kendall if she minded if he stayed until January the second. Kendall was delighted to have him stay, but she checked with Lucille because her house was where he slept every night. Mama assured Kendall that her father was no trouble at all, in fact she was loving the live-in company, and she was dreading the thought of him leaving so soon. Mama was more than happy to have him around for another week.

Kendall told Anthony she would not be surprised if Mama went to visit her father in Phoenix sometime soon. Their friendship was blossoming. Kendall had even heard her father call Lucille, "Mama" a few times and she now referred to Arthur as "Art," which Kendall loved, of course because Kendall knew *her* Art could help troubled hearts heal too.

The family spent the next five days together relaxing and playing with Harper and all her new Christmas toys. Mama, Reign and Kendall spent one morning looking for a wedding dress for

Kendall. She had not purchased one, but she had a few she was considering, none of which had made her cry when she tried them on, which she had heard meant none of them was "the one" yet. She was open to looking for other options. She was shopping from the racks at bridal shops since she needed a dress so quickly. She made one more appointment for the 3rd of January because she couldn't wait too long or a dress she chose couldn't be altered in time. She promised Anthony she wasn't trying to be picky. She knew with her situation she couldn't afford to be. She knew she would find just the right dress at just the right time. She was in a rush yet trying hard to be patient.

Anthony and Kendall had designed and ordered their wedding invitations with rush delivery, but that still was not going to give their guests much notice. They wanted to get married, however, sooner rather than later. They knew that the people that needed to be at the wedding would be there no matter what, with months to plan or with last-minute notice.

Times had certainly changed at Kendall's house. As a result, she and Anthony planned a quiet evening at home for New Year's Eve. Mama and Arthur were joining them, so the two of them spent the day at Mama's house making homemade pizza dough and red pizza sauce to take over to Kendall's house for homemade pizza night. Anthony had also purchased some champagne for everyone. Harper, however, would be having milk, peas, sweet potatoes and bananas, as most babies her age do.

Kendall had chosen a quiet night in because the next day, she was hosting the neighborhood New Year's Day party. She persuaded Peg to let her host, so Harper would be comfortable and still be able to nap in her own bed. Because Kendall was hosting, she included Reign and Branton this year. Peg did not seem to mind the additions.

After pizza and sundown, all five members of her family stepped out into the wintry moonlight to watch fireworks coming from another neighborhood. They enjoyed the fireworks appearing over the tree line, especially because they were free entertainment and far enough away as not to frighten Harper with the loud noises. Cola and Fendy were another story, however. The group couldn't stay outside long because of those two. Cola's ears were very sensitive, and Fendy did not like it whenever people left her alone. They could surely cause destruction together if left alone for long under those conditions in Kendall's house together. In fact, Kendall was already worried Cola might just get into the leftover pizzas they left out on the counter.

As the group walked back toward Kendall's back door, Kendall turned the knob and noticed the door was locked. She swallowed hard, became concerned, and then tried again. Kendall had no key on her or hidden outside anywhere. She immediately asked Anthony to run to check the front door. He came back around the house straight away saying that the front door was locked too. Kendall walked to her bedroom window to check it next. It too was locked. Kendall thought to check the kitchen window over the sink after that. "Anthony, the next window to check is higher off the ground. Can you give me a boost up?" As soon as he got her high enough to see in the window, Kendall screamed and banged on the window and frightened Anthony causing him to almost drop her to the ground. As she tried opening the window, she realized it was *actually* open.

As Kendall opened the window wide enough to fit through, she began to crawl through it explaining to everyone outside waiting about what she had just seen that caused her to yell and startle Anthony, "Cola and Fendy were having a party of their own in the kitchen just as I thought they might. Dang it! Fendy was on top of the counter eating pizza and Cola was on two legs leaning on the counter going to town on the leftover pizza. Her face was *covered* in red sauce when I looked in and started banging. Those stinkers were having their own party until my banging and screaming disrupted it," Kendall quickly slipped into the window and landed in the kitchen sink on top of the dirty dishes.

She jumped out of the sink and ran to the front door to let the others in saying, "Anthony, I'm giving you an extra key for your key chain *before* you leave tonight because you *always* have your keys on you. I do not want that to happen ever again. What if we had left Harper inside? That could have been tragic. And now, I'm sure you will be up all night letting Cola out after *that* late night snack."

As Kendall looked over at Fendy and Cola, she could have sworn she saw them smiling at each other.

Arthur and Mama left shortly after heading inside, cleaning up, and sharing an early toast. Kendall and Anthony were planning to put Harper to bed and ring in the New Year at midnight while watching New Year's Rockin' Eve. Kendall was so excited to have people and specifically a "special someone" to celebrate with this year that she was not about to touch her planner. She had already posted *the list* with lines through every single task on the refrigerator door. She couldn't help but think, if she did make a list this year, what it just might have on it. But then she closed her eyes and thought to herself, "Nah, I don't need a list this year. I already have everything I could want or need, well except for maybe a wedding dress." Her priorities were adjusted, and she had spent the evening with a special someone, the man of her dreams, the true love of her life, and the sweetest little girl imaginable. Both are perfect gifts, true blessings. And she was indeed happy.

Chapter Nineteen

January

Apparently, Harper was ready for the New Year celebration because she was begging to get out of her bed before the sun came up. Kendall had lots of cooking and decorating to do, so she was not at all upset about getting an early start.

Mama showed up early to assist with the party set-up while Kendall ran with Harper to the local convenience store to get a few things like extra napkins and bags of ice. It was the only local store open on the holiday. Kendall was racing around the store pushing Harper in her stroller and carrying one of the store's baskets when she turned down an aisle and bumped into Colin and Cornelia, of all people. They were all stunned to be facing each other in a gas station convenience store, of all places because their last encounter occurred at a country club.

"Hey! I am so sorry I literally bumped into you. We are just here picking up a few things for a party I'm having at the house today. So sorry if I hurt you, Colin."

"No worries, you just clipped my leg," said Colin looking at Harper with his arm around Cornelia. "You are having a party at your house? And who is this here with you? A friend's kid?"

"Actually, this is *my daughter*, Harper. And yes, I'm having my neighborhood buddies over to celebrate the New Year today. I have had one heck of a year this year from losing my mom and my best childhood friend to getting engaged, adopting Harper here, and choosing to close the gallery to stay home with her."

Kendall wanted to say, "And I took Fendy to the vet *all by myself* the other day because she is STILL *alive*, and now my fiancé and I have a *dog*, too," but she didn't dare.

"I am impressed and also sorry to hear about your losses. Congratulations on adopting Harper, meeting someone, and getting engaged! I am so happy for you! It sounds to me like you have really had a year; it seems you have made lots of changes in your life, and they have paid off. Kendall, I am glad we ran into each other again and today of all days. I am glad to know you are happy. You sure do look it. Good to see you! And Happy New Year!" Colin said walking away holding hands with Cornelia.

Kendall felt nothing seeing him this time around. In fact, she was excited that she and Harper had run into them. It was much needed closure. And she was glad she had great developments in her life to share with Colin, even if she did not share them *all* with him. It made her feel proud of herself, not in a bad way, but in a good way. She had come a long way, and it was nice to be able to share just how far, especially with someone who would never have believed it possible one year ago when he had broken her heart by breaking up with her. She knew that sometimes a person's heart has to be broken and put back together to be able to accept the love of another person, the right person, *The One*. Colin had broken hers and Anthony had healed it so that she could love Anthony, Harper and all her new friends like she had never loved before.

Peg came over early just as Kendall got back from the store bringing all her southern New Year food necessities and to see that the party was going the way she always planned it. Peg was lovely, but she liked to be in control, especially of parties. Madge showed up on time with Harry and Larry with a new bouffant hairdo, smelling like gardenias in bloom and carrying her relish tray. Harry brought two liters of cranberry ginger ale to share because it was his very favorite this time of year. Larry came empty handed because Peg had already brought over their contributions. Arthur came over a bit later carrying Mama's crockpot full of meatballs in red sauce, of course. Tish brought her favorite soup and homemade bread again since everyone loved it last year. And Anthony was already in his designated location in the dining room serving each guest their drink of choice along with champagne for toasting.

The group sat down right at one o'clock for a late lunch without Reign and Branton. Kendall had not heard from them the night before or all morning. She was a bit concerned, but she had a house full of guests and the food was getting cold, so she couldn't do anything about her worries in that moment. She wished she had tried to call them earlier before her other company started arriving to confirm that they were indeed planning to show up.

Kendall had just stood up to make the first toast when Branton walked in the front door alone saying, "I am so sorry I am so late. Reign was having lots of pain last night, so we spent last night in the emergency room." Kendall's heart dropped, she was so scared to hear the news, and she almost burst out crying.

"Where is Reign now? How is the baby?" Kendall asked concerned.

"I am right here," said Reign, walking in the door looking like a supermodel with a basketball under her shirt carrying a five-layer coconut cake. "The baby is great. He didn't like the food I ate last night, apparently," she said, dropping the cake off on the buffet table and walking toward the dining table. She and Branton joined everyone at the table as Kendall raised her glass to start her toast once again.

"Well, first off." Kendall looked at Anthony and winked saying, "Told ya, Hon! I won!" Then Kendall turned to Reign and Branton saying, "Cheers to baby boy Fleming. Congrats you two! I'm glad to hear you are having a boy, and that he is all good. Glad you both could join us this year and that you live near us and not all the way in the city."

"To the people around this table— you two, my dad and all of my neighbors who I can now call my friends. --To all of you, thank you for making my life so rich and meaningful. You *all* have supported me in such beautiful ways this year, from friendship, companionship, wisdom offered, to being here to support me and my decision to adopt Harper. Neighbors, you all are like her aunts and uncles now. And, you have all *spoiled* Harper like a family would, as well."

Kendall looked over at the dog asleep next to Harper in her swing and said, "Cola girl, I thank your dad for bringing you into my life. Thanks to you, I have officially become a "dog person." Fendy, you didn't just hear that."

"To Mama, I love you like a mom. I love how you love Anthony and how you have come to love and accept Harper and me, too. I cannot wait until we are officially related."

"To Dad, thanks for being here with us this year. Thanks for all the years just being there, thanks for how you loved mom and how you continue to love me."

"To Anthony, thank you so much for coming into my life the way you did, first as a friend and now as the love of my life. You bring me such joy, and I cannot wait to become your wife and for you to officially become Harper's father in less than a month."

"Thanks again to all of you for helping me through this year. As Ashley Cooke says in one of my favorite songs, "It's Been a Year." And, dang, it has been a year! My mom wanted me to find my happiest happy, and thanks to you all, I have. Ya'll are it! You each bring out the best in me and make me the happiest I have ever been. Much love to you all. If you ask me, this is what friends and family are for—celebrating, supporting, encouraging and enjoying life together."

"One more thing, I want to publicly admit that I will not be making any lists or resolutions this year because I have exactly everything I could want or need, and I am exactly who I want to be doing exactly what I want to do thanks to every one of you, of course. This past year, I made the conscious effort to make room for more joy and for more hope and for more people in my life, and I am glad there was just enough room to fit each and every one of you around this table. Cheers! And Happy New Year! May it be a blessed one for us all." **The End.**

The List   December 31ˢᵗ

1. ~~Get to know the neighbors.~~

2. ~~Reconnect with Cait and meet Harper.~~

3. ~~Go visit Mom and Dad.~~

4. ~~Discover a new emerging artist for the gallery.~~

5. ~~Hire a personal assistant.~~

6. ~~Let Hilda go, so I can clean my own house.~~

7. ~~Meet a real man that loves me like my father loves my mother.~~

8. ~~Spend New Year's Eve next year with a special someone.~~

WHAT A YEAR! SO THANKFUL I MADE ROOM FOR WHAT MATTERS!
Kendall

May *You* Also

MAKE ROOM FOR JOY!

Appendix

RECIPES

Peg's Breakfast Casserole
Kendall's Strawberry Party Cake
Fitzpatrick Family Freezer Ice Cream Custard
Peg's Vegetable Cheese Soup
Peg's Taco Casserole
Mama Leone Recipes

Peg's Breakfast Casserole

8 eggs

1 cup milk

1/2 teaspoon seasoned salt

2 cups shredded hash brown potatoes

1 lb. breakfast sausage

1 cup diced yellow onion

1/2 cup diced red bell pepper

Preheat oven to 350. Brown sausage in a large cast iron skillet. Set it aside. In a large bowl, beat eggs, milk and seasoned salt together. Stir. Put the remaining ingredients into the egg mixture. Save some cheese to sprinkle on top. Pour the egg mixture on top of the sausage. Sprinkle the remaining cheese on top. Bake for 25-30 minutes or until the top is golden brown and a knife inserted near the center comes out clean.

Kendall's Strawberry Party Cake

1 box white cake mix

4 unbeaten eggs

1 box strawberry Jello —3 oz. size dissolved in 1/2 cup   boiling water

3/4 cup salad oil (Crisco or similar)

1/2 box (thawed at room temperature) frozen strawberries—10 oz. size

Mix all well and cook in 2 layer cake pans greased and lined with wax paper. Bake @ 350 for 40 minutes. Remove from pans, cool, then ice with icing/

Icing

Combine one stick margarine or butter, 1 box powdered sugar and the other half box of strawberries and mix until blended and smooth.

Fitzpatrick Family Freezer Ice Cream Custard

Heat 1/2 gallon milk until film appears on top, Separate 5 eggs. Beat yolks, add a small amount of warm milk to eggs and then pour them both into milk. Add 2 1/2 cups sugar, 1/2 tsp. salt. Cook until thickened and coats a wooden spoon. Add one tall can (13oz.) Carnation evaporated milk (chilled). Add vanilla (2tsps.) then other flavor as desired (fruit, etc.). Whip egg whites stiff and fold in. Place in ice cream freezer container (chilled) and freeze.

Peg's Vegetable Cheese Soup

3 Tbsp. butter

1/2 cup each of celery, onion, carrots (chopped however you like) and shredded cabbage

1 cup diced potatoes

8 slices (8oz.) American cheese (not American cheese food)

3 chicken bouillon cubes

Sauté the first 5 ingredients and add 3 chicken bouillon cubes to 1 quart water. Bring all ingredients to a boil and add 1 cup diced potatoes. Simmer for 20 minutes. Add 8 slices American cheese. Melt and stir. Do not boil.

Peg's Taco Casserole

1 1/2 pounds ground beef— brown in skillet and drain. Mix in one packet of Taco Mix seasoning. Then add 1 large (16oz.) can of tomato sauce. Add 1 can of Ranch Style brand beans or any other chili beans will do. Add all cans undrained. Crush some Doritos (crush however many you desire) and add them into mixture. Top with grated cheese. Then stand up some Doritos around in mixture once in casserole dish. Heat for 30 minutes at 325 degrees until bubbling and very hot. Serve with a green salad.

Mama Leone Recipes

Mama Leone would not and could not contribute recipes because as she said, "All of my recipes are total family secrets or rip-offs of famous chefs that I have taken on as my own through the years, so I must not share a one. Please understand!"

Spotify Playlist

MAKING ROOM

1. Seasons of Love—Cast of Rent

2. God Is In This Story—Katy Nichole

3. Canvas—Colton Dixon

4. 9 to 5—Dolly Pardon

5. Peg—Steely Dan

6. Back to Life—Soul II Soul

7. Changes—David Bowie

8. Footloose—Kenny Loggins

9. Almost Paradise—Mike Reno, Ann Wilson

10. St. Patrick's Day—John Mayer

11. Irish Pub Song—The High Kings

12. Art Show—Laura Karpman, Raphael Saadiq

13. Mother Like Mine—The Band Perry

14. Ready To Take a Chance Again—Barry Manilow

15. I Do—Colbie Callait

16. Movin' Out— (Anthony's Song)—Billy Joel

17. Never 'til now—Ashley Cooke, Brett Young

18. Bless the Broken Road—Rascal Flatts

19. September Morn—Neil Diamond

20. You Can't Make Old Friends—Kenny Rogers, Dolly Parton

21. September—Earth, Wind, & Fire

22. Sweetest Devotion—Adele

23. Isn't She Lovely—Stevie Wonder

24. Daughters—John Mayer

25. Monster Mash—Bobby "Boris" Pickett, The Crypt Kickers

26. Joy to the World (Instrumental Version)—The O'Neill Brothers

27. it's Been a year—Ashley Cooke

28. That's What Friends Are For—Dionne Warwick, Elton John, Gladys Knight, Stevie Wonder

29. Auld Lang Syne — Guy Lombardo

30. Making Room — Paul Eerhart

About the Author

Mandy Miller is both a writer and an artist. She started writing and painting as her children grew up and "flew" the nest. She enjoys creating stories about growth and change and joy and hope with a little humor mixed in along the way. She has written several novels, children's books using her paintings and photography as illustrations, as well as art books describing what and why she paints. She lives in Tennessee with her husband and two dogs. If she is not out enjoying nature, she is certainly reading, writing or painting in her studio.

Mandy-Miller-Studio.com

instagram.com/mandymillerstudio

instagram.com/mandymillerauthor

Cover Design by Spencer Miller— instagram.com/spencermil ler

Made in United States
Orlando, FL
14 October 2024

52653154R10127